DANAE SAMSON

Author Photo: Leah Samson-French

Born in Southern California and educated in Portland, Oregon, Danae Samson received her Bachelors and Masters degrees from Portland State University and went on to teach English at three colleges in California and Washington. Deciding to pursue writing full time, Danae began work on…

LAMENT HILL,

which is her debut novel and first published work. Danae Samson lives in Riverside, California, USA.

For more forthcoming titles from
MEDIAARIA CDM visit
www.mediaaria-cdm.co.uk

**MediaAria CDM
Proudly Presents…**

Lament Hill

by

Danae Samson

MEDIAARIA CDM LTD

MediaAria CDM Ltd, Business Correspondence:
14 Paget Road, Oxford OX4 2TD, United Kingdom

www.mediaaria-cdm.co.uk

This novel is a work of fiction and,
any resemblance to actual persons, living or
dead, is entirely coincidental.

This work is published by
MediaAria CDM Ltd 2011

Copyright © Danae Samson 2011

**The Author asserts the moral right to be
identified as the author of this work**

First Edition

Cover Art by Jess Sully

All rights reserved. No part of this publication may be
reproduced, stored in a retrieval system, or transmitted,
in any form or by any means, electronic, mechanical,
photocopying, recording or otherwise, without the prior
permission of the publisher.

ISBN 978-0-9565316-6-7

MediaAria CDM Ltd is commited to a sustainable future
for our publishing industry, readers and our planet.
Further information can be found at
www.mediaaria-cdm.co.uk/About-Us

Manufactured in the United Kingdom.

This work is dedicated to my uncle,
Dr Steven Wickler.
The handsome, geeky horse doctor who intrigued me as a child, inspired me as an adult and who taught me that intelligence is best displayed through a sense of humour. Love and miss you, Uncle Steve.

CHAPTER ONE

*D*avid exhaled warm air into the dampness and watched as it turned into a thick white cloud before disappearing.

"Cold," he shivered.

"Yeah, can't seem to shake it," Brian said, holding his knees to his chest.

"How ya feelin'?"

"Tired, my freakin' back is killing me."

David looked at his friend, his six foot frame bundled into a ball, his face aged ten years by the last couple of days. The tree was protecting them for the most part, but occasionally a raindrop fell from its branches onto Brian's pale face. His hair was wet and his clothes clung to his shivering body.

"It's the coughing. I think you've got pneumonia."

"That figures. Pretty nice trip you've planned here, asshole."

"Hey! You wanted to hike, jerk-off. Don't blame me." David's face felt warm, his head angry.

"Well how the hell did you get us lost then? You said you knew the way!"

"Brian, knock it off, okay. We're lost, that's it, so just fucking chill out. Rangers will come."

"It's been three days! Nobody is coming!" Tears began to fall down his cheek, colliding with the raindrops. "We're gonna fuckin' die out here."

"No, we're not." David's voice rattled with the chills that swept throughout his body. He was cold, hungry, and scared. They should have found them by now.

"Why don't you go try to find the road. I'll stay right here and-"

"No," David snapped, "I'm not going off and leaving you like this."

"But if you try, then one of us might make it."

"Drop it, Bri, I'm not going! We'll stay and wait. Someone will come."

"But what if we both die?" The tears were rolling in streams, bloodshot eyes pleading for sleep, food, warmth, anything.

David turned to Brian and gripped both his shoulders. "I'm not leaving and we're not going to die," David's arms embraced Brian's head and his cheek registered its temperature. "Oh Jesus, you're burn' up."

"I'm sorry, D. I didn't want to tell you, think I'm in real trouble, man."

"Okay, okay, just hang in. C'mon buddy, you can do it. Just sit tight."

Brian nodded and then sprung from David's embrace to expel a cough that bellowed through the forest air. David smacked his back, but the coughing continued. Veins pushed from underneath the surface of Brian's skin and his neck looked as if it would burst under their pressure. His back arched and collapsed in steady jerks and jolts until the spasms ceased. He returned to his position against the tree's massive trunk, exhausted.

"Can't take this, D. So tired, feels like my chest is being squeezed."

"I know, I know. Just breathe, Bri, slowly breathe." David pulled Brian's back to his chest and tried to make his friend more comfortable. Their body heat barely penetrated Brian's soaked clothes. David's jacket and pants had been the better choice, light, but waterproof, and beneath their surface David had a layer of dry long-johns.

"Get up." David said, standing.

"What? What the fuck for?"

"I'm giving you my clothes, now get up."

"D, no. I'm already screwed, but if you get sick then we're up the creek."

"We're not up a creek and stop talking like my granny. They will find us, but until then we have to keep you warm."

David shed his top layer and used the jacket to protect the dry clothes as he exchanged with Brian. When they were finished, Brian remained standing and shifted his weight from side to side.

"Better?"

"Much, thanks."

"You'd do it for me. Fuck I'm cold!" David laughed and Brian smiled. David couldn't help but notice the intense weakness that covered Brian's face.

"Maybe it is time to head out."

Brian's head snapped up. "Yeah, yeah man, absolutely. I'm totally fine now and can just wait-"

"No, I mean, we should both go, right now. The sun is already up and we need to make the most of the light."

"I don't think I can."

"Well, you have to. Let's go." David began out into the rain. The flesh of his back rippled in gooseflesh from the moisture and his body stiffened against the cold.

"D!"

David turned. His friend looked so old and fragile.

"What if we don't make it?"

"Then at least we won't die alone."

Sunlight streamed through the freshly cleaned window, revealing the remaining dust on a cluttered desk. The rhythmic repetition of fingers busy at their keyboard divided the quiet in small choppy bursts. The flow slowed and abruptly stopped.

"C'mon on, dummy."

Running his smooth fingers through his hair, David Masterson teetered on the back two legs of his office chair. His desktop cursor blinked indifferently, marking the passing minutes.

"What would you do? What would *he* do?" David leveled his chair and reread the last two lines. "Girls, minors, booze, room." The answer felt close. "Dumb shit," he said with slight amusement.

"One born every minute." a voice replied.

David looked up to find the lanky silhouette of his editor blocking the doorway.

"You know, Martin, for having been in the business for a thousand years, you have very little compassion for the struggling musician."

"You're kidding, right? Those struggling musicians spend more money on cat food than we do on rent. It's their own goddamn fault for, what was it with this one? Highballs and a fender bender? Asshole squared."

Martin's abrasive words often made him unpopular with the LA crowd, but the rock and rollers, like David, appreciated his honesty. No bullshit and lace, as far as he was concerned.

"Did you want something?" David asked, still amused.

"Jared Lucas. Wants to do a six page intimate."

"Are you serious?"

"Yeah, says he's ready. Says he wants you to do it."

"What? Why me? I mean, I've never done anything over two pages and that's counting the photos."

"I know. I don't understand it, but he says he's been following your work and feels that you would have a better understanding of what he has to say, whatever the fuck that means."

Martin stood with his back pressed against the wall, arms crossed, eyes looking past David to the small window. He squinted at the incoming light, which David thought made him look older than his fifty-five years.

David's mind began to spin. He had only been with *Wolf* Magazine a year come February and here it was only late October. He had done pieces on the local music scene and a few phone interviews with a couple new up and comers, but it usually ended up being a collection of his limited observations, such as his present project.

"I don't have the background, Martin. I can't do a six page intimate, Lucas will eat me alive. He's supposed to be a freakin' nightmare and crazy as all hell-"

"No," Martin said pushing off of the wall, "you will do it. You'll kick that Andrew's piece down to Jake, go home and pack and be on a plane to Oregon tomorrow morning."

David looked overwhelmed. Martin sensed his nervousness and backed off.

"Look, this is a huge assignment and you'll be carrying the magazine on your shoulders. But, if you do a good job, we can talk promotion, set you up in a bigger office with a little more cash. I need a good writer, Dave. Ever since Kelly left, our up close and personals have been suffering. If you can make this work, I'll give you your head start." He gave David a pat on the shoulder, "could have an actual career here, sport. Stop living with your parents."

"Very funny, Marty."

"I told you to watch that Marty shit, asshole," Martin looked irritated, but David knew the jab was fair game. Martin was, after all, feeding him to the lions. "Oregon, tomorrow. Call me when you get in. Don't blow it." He headed towards the door and just before it closed David caught him.

"Martin, what about Lucas? I mean, I've heard he's crazy. No female reporter will go near him."

"Yeah, it's true, but this is his first interview in five years and we got it. All he does is stay up in the mountains, writing and recording. He's never had to go back on tour because his record sales are so incredible. He's a recluse, a private man who definitely has his qualms with the world." Their eyes met, David's young and wide and Martin's strong and focused. "So," he started again, breaking their stare, "wipe your feet before entering, close the door when you leave and don't piss him off. Its several miles from his place to the nearest neighbor and most of that is condensed forest. Got it?"

"Ah, yeah."
"Good. Best of luck. And David?"
"Hmm?"
"Be careful."

*

Masterson unlocked the door to his hot two-bedroom apartment. His entrance was slow as he watched for his furry roommate. A few feet away an orange shape emerged from the living room.
"Hey, Horatio."
The feline strutted towards his owner and allowed himself to be hoisted up and cradled.
"Any messages?"
He slowly made his way through the room, flipping on a series of lights and rummaging through the daily mail. Though hot, the loft-like apartment was clean and spacious. David had been lucky to obtain it as the neighborhood was nice and the rent was decent. The previous tenant had been his ex-girlfriend who had wished to turn it into a dancing studio. Funds fell through, as did their relationship and she had given it to him as an apology, an apology perhaps for giving up, for leaving or for loving his best friend. He had always thought the worst of the three. Melissa was a good woman, beautiful, smart, and he had blown it. Blown it and ruined what could have been marriage. He had begged her to take him back, she had refused, and promptly married Brian. He had forgiven them, they had forgiven him and then they left for Colorado.
It was after she left that he began writing for magazines. His success in freelancing gave him a confidence that teaching never had. After a year out in the field, he was recruited by Martin's assistant, who introduced him to Martin. A week later he was given a closet sized office, a desk, telephone and a mailbox number. It seemed to have all come so fast

and up until now David felt he could handle it. Until now.

Jared Lucas. The name itself was coated in power and mystery and the owner, from what David had heard, was just as strange. After Martin had left his office, David had begun an afternoon of research on the famous musician. He found the basics:
birth-date, education, family, first gig, first record, etc. Lucas had married in his mid twenties, but by the time his fortieth birthday rolled around the couple had divorced. She now lived in Utah with her mother and he had built a house in Oregon. He toured for eight more years, returned to his mountain retreat and never came out. That was five years ago. When the news broke of his possible retirement, Lucas replied not with a press conference, but with the release of a new album. On the inside cover he very plainly stated, "Be happy with this and don't ask for a tour". The fans rallied and the album went triple platinum. This odd communication continued in a six-month cycle for five years. News of Lucas' retirement, an album release and a denial of any appearances.

David collapsed in the cool sheets of his bed and let his eyes rise to the ceiling. Not quite a long day, as tomorrow would be longer and no doubt with more surprises. It was an opportunity he knew, but the weight was undeniably overwhelming. Jared Lucas had followed his work. And what work would that be? His small articles on the big city's nightclubs and local coffee houses? Hardly, he thought, worth reading outside a bathroom. His position at *Wolf* of course had provided greater opportunities and the clientele had risen to a higher scale of Californian celebrity, but nothing extraordinary. Certainly Lucas must have other reasons.

David's eyes slowly began to black out and he fell deeper into the embracing mattress. His mind shifted from the white walls of his studio ceiling into a darkness that gradually came into focus. He was standing in a small clearing among draping trees, their long, drooping branches softly hung in an early morning twilight. His feet were bare, snapping small twigs as he walked. The sun hadn't quite risen and darkness was still clinging to the last minutes of night. David eased through the cool trees spaciously placed and suddenly stopped to find a dark object in front of him. Hanging from what David thought to be the creature's feet, hung a man-shaped being. His ankles strapped together with rope, the creature hung upside down with his back to where David stood. David looked on for only a second before the creature snapped around to face him. His bright blue eyes were wide and vibrant among the nest of black hair that covered its entire body. He looked at David, those eyes clear and terrifying.

"Tend to your troubles," it said, "be mindful of the red plum, not true but wicked . . . wicked falling stars." He seemed to reach for David, but his arms hung without movement at his sides. "Not to rest, not to rest, peaceful mind."

David sprung from his mattress and straight into the empty room air. His chest heaved and his sheets sank from his sweat.

"Sweet Jesus."

At the foot of his bed Horatio raised his head in irritation. David stroked the feline's coarse hair along his mane, trying to soothe himself more than the animal and lay back down. He was never one for nightmares. Any hidden aggression or conflict he had was often, and unfortunately for others, vented through his writing. He did not believe in holding on to something that was only going to eat you up in the long run. But now, in the early morning shadows he felt his brain ache with a faint humming from the presence of something that was gone now but had been present shortly before. A visitor. A visitor, who had come, rattled his cage and left. And who, David felt very confidently, would be back.

CHAPTER TWO

David hated airports, always had. The rush and rumble of an overpopulated place cluttered by baggage and jet-lagged travelers always seemed to put him in a bad mood. He never understood the frequent flyer. Someone traveling for business or pleasure that spent most of their god given time on an airplane and the rest of it in a noisy epicenter such as this one. The key, David figured, was to have a secured plan as to avoid any traveling interruptions. He had mastered his own form of travel by the time he was eighteen. Drive always if possible, fly only if necessary. Portland was not far, but his invitation to Jared Lucas's home stood only for the weekend and Martin had not given him a traveling option.

David passed through security with his laptop and personal knapsack, walked to his gate, and twenty minutes later boarded his flight. He entered through the oval archway and exchanged greetings with a blonde flight attendant.

"There is assigned seating, but if you wish to change seats once the final boarding call is made, please feel free to do so," She recited. David thought her smile looked like some accessory she put on in the morning along with her earrings and makeup. He made his way down the narrow aisle to the seat marked D34. The plane was delightfully empty and within the first section David counted only seven other passengers. The airport plague began to dissipate and he nuzzled into his seat by the window. A yawn escaped his lips out into the concealed plane. It was still early and the sun wasn't even up yet. He felt his head begin to roll when a voice made him snap it back up.

"Wouldn't do dat if I was you."

David turned and saw a petite, old, black woman standing in the center aisle. Her hands clutched a large carpetbag that made her look child size in comparison. "I'm sorry, uh. . . . wouldn't do what?" David asked.

"I wouldn't seep on da plane. People have bad dreams when dhey fly."

David was amused. "Well, I've always been able to sleep anywhere." He said giving her his best respect-thy-elders-smile.

"Not gonna listen to me are ya?" she smiled back. "Well, okay. S'pose its best for you to getta feel early on anyhow. So, go on ahead. Take a little nap. May be one of the best lessons ya'll ever learn."

"Ma'am, I don't know," he started, but she had already continued down the row. David arched out of his seat just in time to see her take a place in the center section Her head momentarily vanished behind the tall cushioned backs, but then briefly popped out from the side long enough to give him a wink before disappearing again. David slid back into his seat. I'll sleep tonight, he thought, but as the plane began to climb David's head slowly lowered.

"It was so unbelievable, Marie. I just stood in complete shock."

Despite the illuminated fasten seatbelt signs, two flight attendants stood talking, blocking the lavatory. A tall brunette with delicate features spoke eagerly attempting to keep her excitement to a whisper. The entranced opposite was older, shorter, and resembled a husky waitress that could be found in bars across the Midwest. The coupled pair of eyes remained fixated on each other as the tall beauty spoke.

"We haven't been trying, I mean, we hadn't planned on it, but I know Chris will be excited. We've been married five years now and I think the timing is good,"

"Um, miss!" a squeaky voice interrupted from the aisle.

"Yes, sir. I'll be just one minute. So, I think I'm going to wait until I get home to tell him because-"
"Miss."
The brunette turned to see the strained face of a small child, no more than ten years old begin to shake with the onset of tears.
"What is it, sweetie?"
"I think that man is sick or something!"
He extended his index finger in the direction of a nearby window seat where David sat twitching and mumbling. With elongated strides the attendant reached David's seat in seconds. His hands were coiled up to his chest and spasmed in rhythmic waves. His head lolled back and forth across the seat's headrest, exposing the inner pinkness of his gaping mouth from several angles. The attendant spoke with calm severity.
"Sir! Wake up sir!"
David's eyelids fluttered at first and then abruptly opened, wide and glassy.
"Are you okay, sir?" she asked.
"What?" He looked at her first in question and then with embarrassed annoyance. "Is there a problem?" His eyes held her hard and unforgiving.
"I, um, the little boy thought you needed help. So, I came to check on you but-"
"Most people don't need help sleeping, do they?" David snapped.
She recoiled from his seat and back into the aisle. Her once brightened face now hung in beaten hurt.
"It was not my intention," she began, but David had already returned to his restful hunch against the window. The attendant stood for a moment in stilled coldness. She felt the tears threatening to come. Why had he been so rude, she thought. You can't lose it here, her mind spoke as her feet began flight down the aisle. She had only gone a few rows when a hand touched her side. She looked down into the eyes of an old black woman.

"Its ayre, love. He didn't mean ta hurt ya." Her smile was warm and gentle and made its way across the short distance to embrace the trembling figure in the aisle.

"I didn't do anything wrong. He was shaking, badly. I wasn't sure..."

"I know ya weren't, honey and its got notang ta do with ya. He just had himself a bad dream. T'ese thangs happen, ya know."

The striking brunette swam in the woman's words and slowly began to feel calm again.

"I'll apologize when he gets off the plane. He'll be rested by then," she whispered. No tears waited now, only a soothing warmth that rocked her.

"Better not, child." the old woman said. "He's not of his own right now. Best ta send your thoughts in prayer."

"Yes, prayer," the attendant sleepily agreed. "Thank you, Mama Legna." Her voice spoke in natural response and she would later try to recall if the old woman had actually given that name.

Mama Legna watched the young woman pass the threshold into the coach, closing a curtain behind her. Checking her beloved carpetbag for safe storage below her seat, Mama Legna rose into the aisle and began to walk. Her height denied her and it wasn't until she was standing in front of his row that she was able to see David's sleeping head. Looking right to left once again, she leaned forward and placed a cold palm onto David's forehead. The skin beneath blazed with heated perspiration. His chest heaved momentarily then released into a heavy sigh.

"Hold fast, my boy. I am here."

"Staaaaaayyyy," he begged, his eyes remaining closed but his face tightening into lines.

"Can't, child. Dis must be done. Face it, face yourself. And I will be waiting for you."

She withdrew her hand, moistened by his sweat.

"Go with god," she whispered.

CHAPTER THREE

Portland International Airport was just as David had left it two years prior. Unusually quiet and clean for a place of constant travel with a view from its top level parking that would rival most in his beloved California. He took a deep breath, inhaling not only the cool air, but the scenery as well and couldn't help but be grateful to Martin for sending him here. He had forgotten what a beautiful city it was. The landscape coated in greenery only to divide for the bridges leading into downtown. He rested against his suitcase, absorbing his surroundings and wondering about his host. Why would one leave such a city for the cold confines of Mt. Hood? He looked to the East and saw a snow covered crescent reaching into the clear sky until its edges came to a point.

"Looks kinda shaky," he said aloud as if the scenery would agree with him, but instead only alerted himself to the situation of time. He glanced at his wrist and decided a trip into downtown would have to wait. He wanted to make it up the mountain before the sun passed beyond the hills dragging the light with it. He took a last look at the view before heading to the rental car station. The sky was a warm blue without a cloud to plague it. It isn't true, he thought, even in October Oregon can have clear skies. But just as any local could tell him, David knew those days were numbered.

David approached the rental car counter to find a young strawberry blonde partially hidden behind a glowing computer screen. She looked up and smiled.

"I have a reservation. Masterson."

"Okay. Let me see... ah, yes. Looks like a Durango with four wheel drive, Friday morning through Sunday evening."

She clicked and pecked until a nearby printer came to life.

"Would you like the insurance?"

"No, my policy will cover it." *Although,* he thought, *if you want me to buy the moon, I will, beauty.*

Her eyes suddenly shot up and for a moment her smile revealed knowledge and a girlish delight at having it.

"That won't be necessary," she grinned. "We probably won't have rain until late next week and the snow is still very high up. Not a huge chance for an accident."

David stood stunned. *Did she hear me?* His mind squirmed. *You didn't tell her you were going up the mountain.*

"How did you know I was going up to Mt. Hood?" he asked, his eyes searching her.

"Four wheel drive, champ. You wouldn't need it otherwise." And there it was again. That smile. The sides of her peach lips rose to the corners of her cheeks in childlike mischief.

The printer stilled and she withdrew four forms from it, the top three bearing credit card numbers and driver's license info and the fourth yielding a map of the mountain.

"Okay," she said, leaning over the fourth page with a red marker. "We are here, take this highway all the way through Troutdale, and the exit to Hood is shortly after that."

David's eyes shifted from her neckline back to her face. He could smell her. Sleep's sweet scent that held her body when she woke that morning. The glaze of a hot shower. And beyond that her perfume already mixing with her body's warmth. It seemed to him that forever had passed since the scent of a woman enveloped him so intensely. When his eyes finally gave sight, there again the smile waited.

"Right," he said pulling himself from the counter. "Through Troutdale. Won't miss it."

The girl did not respond. Her grin widened.

"Better split," he said managing a shaky smile. He bent for his bags and rose to find the girl in front of him.

"Don't forget this, champ. Wouldn't want to get lost up there. Rangers never search private properties."

She held the map out to him and he quickly took it and a step backward.

"Thanks. Why, about the rangers?"

She inched forward and for a moment David felt his heart slow. The smile gone, her face hung in youthful solace.

"I wouldn't waste on worrying about them. Rangers are useless anyway. The ones who get out always find their own way."

Her glance fell downward.

"Not everyone has the strength to do that you know. Not everyone can find their way. I mean, that's why they call it being lost, right?" She looked at him pushing an answer.

"Sure. I guess." he said.

"When the time comes, you won't have to." Her face seemed to fill his entire field of vision and a cold crossed him.

David nodded and turned. He decided he would stop on the way and make a copy of the map, or perhaps two, just to be safe.

CHAPTER FOUR

Rain had begun to fall by the time David's Durango reached the entrance to Mt. Hood. The temperature was still pleasant and the light drops of rain refreshed David's thoughts. Jared Lucas. "Musician, genius, recluse, alone," the correlating words streamed into each other as David tried to find his angle. His inner writing pen began to stride. "Jared Lucas leads a solitary life in the deep forests of Mt. Hood, Oregon. Lucas took to his fifty-four acre estate five years ago following the completion of his tenth album, *Falling*." Not bad, he thought. The opening line was solid, but the second sentence said nothing as to the article's purpose. David's great Aunt Dee was a romance novelist for thirty years and yielded what David thought was the greatest literary advice he had ever been given. "By the second line is on time." As always, she had been right. There was nothing that frustrated an abbreviated reader (Martin's nickname for *Wolf* faithfuls, people only interested in under two page literature) more than an article without immediate explanation. Within a glance a purpose should be found. It was sad, but true and David was just grateful to his beloved aunt for teaching him to know better.

The road was clear and for the most part abandoned aside from the occasional mountain biker. The Durango steadily climbed its way to moderate elevation. Bob Seger was singing about rollin' away. She had taken all his Bob Seger albums. Where had they been? In the kitchen?

"You don't even listen to them anymore, David."

"Doesn't matter, they're mine! Tell Brian to get his own damn music!"

"Can we not do this. I just want to get the rest of my

things and go."

"Fine. Take the Segers and the Beatles and all the rest of it!" He walked into her space and breathed on her forehead. "I don't want anything you've ever touched. Now get the hell out."

She grabbed the box of vinyl and left. He ran to the sink and vomited. The concentrated smell of alcohol made his eyes water. Even now a twinge of that smell seemed to invade his senses.

After an hour the Durango left the main road for a private drive. There were houses, fronted by mailboxes and ridiculously long driveways. Behind the layers of trees David could see the outlines of moss covered roofs and smoking chimneys. He looked at the directions Martin had given him, deduced it would not be long and decided to phone him. A series of beeps hummed at his ear before Martin's voice picked up the line.

"Hey, boss. Almost there."

"Good. You better not be pissin' around downtown. I told Lucas you would be there by lunch, it's already passed 11:00, asshole."

"Yeah, I know, but I'm on Moldy Drive right now and should be reaching the Lucas looney bin any minute."

"That's enough, smart ass. I mean what I said. Don't go fucking around with Lucas, he doesn't like it. And if he decides to bury you under a log somewhere out in BFE I'm not flying up there to find your stupid ass. Got it?"

The Durango came to a stop in front of black rod iron gates with the words *Lament Hill* arched across their peaks.

"Oh, sorry honey, gotta go. Kiss the kids."

"Bite me."

Martin's voice was replaced by a dull dial tone. David grinned and got out of the car. He hadn't realized when he first saw them, but the gates themselves stood fifteen feet in height where they met stone pillars on each side and at least twenty feet at their center. *Lament Hill.* Each letter written in a bold, medieval script that seemed both intentionally endearing and modestly simple. He stood for a moment, gazing as if at a statue and jumped when the word *Lament* broke from its partner granting entrance to the obviously coveted *Hill*. David returned to the waiting Durango and proceeded forward. The sides of the road dropped into dark gullies leaving just enough room on the road for two cars. The gates closed behind the Durango, once again forming the tall, impenetrable iron guardian. David drove slowly along the well-pressed dirt road, which quickly gave way to a brick driveway. He looked for a house, but only saw dense forest in every direction. Strange, he thought, so early in the day and there is hardly any light, rather dark, actually. Had he brought his flashlight? Yes, along with a rain slicker and waterproof boots. His camping trip a couple years prior had taught him never to visit Oregon's beautiful mountains without the proper supplies. Almost died that trip, but luckily the road had been closer than they thought. He was lucky that time, but planned never to be unprepared again. His thoughts entranced him and it wasn't until the very last moment that he suddenly braked to avoid hitting a man in the road. David's heart caught in his chest, skipped a beat, and then thumped wildly under a rush of adrenalin. The man was tall, dark complexioned, and stared dully at the shaken figure behind the wheel. He walked around the front of the vehicle and approached the driver's side window. David lowered it, stuttering apologies.

"It's alright, son. I saw you enter the gate. Had a feeling you might not be looking at the road, seeing as how there's so much more to look at."

His eyes were gentle, his hair slightly grayed and thick.

"I am very sorry," David stammered. "I'm here to visit Mr. Lucas, he's expecting me."

"Yes, I know," He grinned with slight amusement. "We don't have many visitors here and the ones that come are very special indeed." He examined David a little before speaking again. "Mr. Lucas is waiting for you. Best get a move on, son. Daylight is short in these parts."

David nodded and shifted the Durango in drive.

"Just follow the path up to the house. That's really the only thing you can do any way." He let out a heavy chuckle and started to walk up the road. "Welcome to Lament Hill, Mr. Masterson." He spoke without turning around.

David let out a sigh to calm his nerves and once again set forth on the red drive.

The house was inarguably grand, huge in size, and posh in style. The old English architecture stood profound against the rugged landscape and David couldn't help but wonder how much money and trouble had gone into its construction. It was not the typical wood and cement compilation, but in lieu a vast mound of stone and brick, obviously sincere to Lucas' British heritage.

David parked his car in the home's circular drive, stopping short of the carport's protective roof. This was not David's house and he did not intend to make himself at home until asked to do so. His Durango was close to the front door, but not in the way of other possible vehicles and not taking a presumptuous place that might land him on Lucas' sour side. This was good, he thought, the small things always matter most.

"Best behavior," he said aloud, smirking at his own cautious tone.

Wide elongated steps that presented the front door like a trophy, fronted the house. Its broad dark-wood surface contrasted with the step's brick red color; David knocked on the mammoth door twice and stepped back. The hinges creaked as the door slowly opened. Behind it an awkward adolescent stood, hair in braids and body clothed in a simple floral dress and tights.

"Can I help you?" she asked, her voice telling David that adolescent was probably a premature title. This girl was more along the lines of seven or eight years old.

"I'm David Masterson. I'm here to see Mr. Lucas."

The girl eyeballed him from toe to top. She looked directly into his eyes, her face so stern and serious that a nervous laugh escaped him and he felt his face turn hot with embarrassment.

"This way," she said leaving the door open for him to pass through. "You can leave your stuff here." She pointed at his overnight knapsack and then at the floor.

The foyer gave way to several halls and two staircases. The girl led him down two steps into a living-room area where David could see shelves of books, awards, candles, and metallic objects that glistened in the room's limited light. They walked through an enormous butler's pantry into a den. The room was dark and it wasn't until after a few moments that David saw Lucas. He was standing in front of a raging fireplace with one hand on its mantle. He turned, his face illuminated by the light, and outstretched a hand to David.

"Well, now, you've made it. How wonderful." He shook David's hand with an eager ferocity that David could see was not intentional. "I had hoped you would be here in time for lunch and here you are . . . in plenty of time."

"It's a pleasure, Mr. Lucas. I love your work."

"Do you now . . . hmmm, I was under the impression that you were more of a Dylan fan."

His accent was clipped and cool, pronouncing each word with strong syllabic emphasis.

"I, ah, I like you both," he managed, releasing Lucas' hand and dropping his eyes a bit.

They stood for a minute. David could feel Lucas'

narrow eyes looking him over, checking his hair, freshly shaven face, and starched collar. Yes, these were the types of things Jared Lucas was known to look for and David was prepared. A quick shave in PDX's restroom after his flight was all he had needed to be ready for this moment.

"You have a beautiful home, Mr. Lucas." David's voice sounded unbelievably loud in the room's silence.

"Yes, thank you. I've worked very hard to make it so." Clipped and cool.

Lucas looked at him one last time then turned to sit on a nearby couch. He spread his arms across its black leather back and nestled into its oversized cushions. David took an opposing seat on a nearby ottoman and waited for an invitation to speak.

"Ever been to Oregon, David?"

"Yeah, my last trip was a couple of years ago, but I try and make it up as much as possible. Escape from the city and everything, you know."

David realized he was wringing his hands in a nervous circular motion and forced himself to stop. An immediate smirk of amusement lifted the corners of Lucas' mouth.

"Yes, I suppose one does need a break from time to time," he said, his smirk growing. "Sadly, this visit will be a working one, but perhaps another, on a later date, can be arranged, one more socially inclined, shall we say."

"Thank you, I would like that." *Actually, I wouldn't. Not with this guy. Roll me away.*

"Right."

His smile now dominated Lucas' fine features and David felt as if it would consume him whole if he looked too long at it. So many teeth. Perfectly aligned, white and slightly jagged. He looked as if he could tear a man to pieces with them.

"Well?"

"Well, what, Mr. Lucas?" His minded had wandered

and the lapse in conversation had been noticed.

"Would you like to ask me a few things?" His voice was high and mocking. "You've come all this way, certainly there is one question in particular that need be asked."

He extended his arm over the end of the sofa allowing his fingers to grab a silver tin that rested on a rod iron end table. He lifted the lid and pulled out a black cigarette and silver lighter. He didn't offer one to David, but instead lit his and returned the tin to its previous place.

"Go on," he said, blowing dark fog toward the ceiling. "Ask. I promise not to take offense."

What question was that? David thought. Only one? What one? His mind raced, mentally sorting through the newspapers and articles he had read. What would anybody take offense to? Something personal, he decided.

"Why did you get divorced?"

"David, no, no, no, not me tosser. You. Ask me a question about you."

"What do I need to know about myself?"

"Plenty. Everybody has something and it changes. Year after year the questions begin to stack up and pretty soon towards the end we can't even remember the first one. Surely, you can't, but there is one that's been thumpin' around in that brain of yours for two days now."

"Why did you choose me?"

"Now, see! That's what I'm talking about!" He clapped his hands together in satisfaction. "We've never met, I don't know you and you don't know me, but I knew what you didn't know about yourself. See?"

"I read you were into philosophy. This is probably where that degree in psych comes in handy." David felt foolish. Why had Martin sent him here?

"Oh, know about that, hmm? Most people don't. You must be very good at what you do."

They exchanged a heavy stare. David was rushed with the need to leave the room, but managed to suppress it. He could do this. He had done it a dozen times before. Jared Lucas was just another arrogant, self-loving, rock star jackass and David could handle him. That's right, handle him all the way to his new office at *Wolf*.

"So, why me?"

"You don't know?"

"No. I don't have the experience for-"

"You think the only experience that matters is the kind derived from your job?"

"No, but for this type of-"

"I didn't ask for you because you're some hot-ass journalist from some wanker magazine. I asked for you because your time has come and we simply must get on with it."

David's face contorted. "I don't understand."

"Dear boy," Lucas leaned forward and placed a pointed elbow on each knee. "You've arrived."

David could feel his skin inching in quick ripples, repelling from the bones beneath its quivering surface. "Yes, I have," he decided to say, "I've arrived here at your house to interview you. Am I wrong?"

Lucas hesitated for a moment, reclined back against the sofa and took a long drag from his cigarette.

"You must be hungry." He said, rising from the couch. "Drake has made lunch for us. I assume you two already met in the yard?"

"Mr. Lucas, why am I here?"

David stood to deliver the question face to face with its intended receiver, but quickly wished he were still sitting. Jared Lucas had the eyes of an abandoned house, windows filled with the light of ghosts residing inside. Those windows stared open at David, holding him.

"Lunch first, then I'll show you the studio."

CHAPTER FIVE

Jared Lucas' kitchen was dark with floor to ceiling stained glass windows restricting the dull mid day light peaking in from outside. On the far side of the room was a long black table, slightly raised as if built to accommodate male stature. Upon the table Drake had placed a large plate of sliced meat, cheese, and vegetables as well as a basket filled with baguettes and oversized rolls. Lucas casually strolled across the terracotta tile and slid into one of the high-backed chairs, his back to the magnificent window. Looking at him, David felt his mind taking in this scene of color contrasting – Lucas' black silhouette sitting upright against the window's background of color, creating a dark hole amid the vibrancy. He appeared to David almost diabolical, as if intentionally ruining the window's beauty.

"Come, sit, young David. You must be famished."

David joined his host at the table, selecting the chair directly opposite him, immediately becoming aware that eye contact would be unavoidable no matter where his eyes fell.

"Drake is wonderful," Lucas began. "He creates the most amazing suppers, but does not favor lunchtime, hence today's display," he said pointing to the platter of meat.

"No, no, it looks great."

David's eyes shifted from the platter to Lucas and then back to the table again.

"I haven't eaten since five," his hands reached for the rolls, "and I love sandwiches. It's the one homemade meal I've managed to perfect."

"Ah, yes, the bachelor's diet. I'm afraid I'm all thumbs with this sort of thing. After my wife and I divorced, I dined out every day until I hired Drake."

"How long has he worked for you?"

"Since I've been here, five years now. His wife passed some time ago and his daughter lives on the East coast. Very simple man, very gracious. He was the first and the last person I interviewed for the position."

They exchanged rolls and condiments as they spoke, occasionally taking bites in between responses. He had been happy here these past five years and went on to say that he would never return to the "outside world".

"What about your fans?"

"What about them?" he said, his head slightly lowered behind the sandwich in his hands.

"Well, I know that they would really respond to even the smallest public appearance."

"No."

"I'm not saying outside of your home even, you could do a TV interview, maybe satellite or something,"

"Out of the question, mate."

"Why?"

"I'm done with that. I never wanted it anyway. People around me all the time, in my home, in my car, in my face," the volume of his voice began to rise, "no respect, no privacy . . . ever!"

His last word hung in the air and David elected to let it go. He had only been here half an hour . . . half an hour and he had screwed up the whole weekend. He went for his napkin in his lap and was about to bring it to the table, pre his departure when Lucas spoke.

"I came up here to save the music, not to hurt my fans. I couldn't create in that environment, I don't know how I ever did, but I did and now that time is over. Here is where I can do what they appreciate. And so it is here that I will stay, for them, and for me."

"I didn't mean anything by it."

"How is your sandwich?"

"It's delicious," David whispered. He felt his

forehead break its previously heated state with a cool relief that sent a small droplet of sweat down his right cheek. Lucas was looking past him now, staring at the window's reflected colors that covered the kitchen's white walls. He did not blink for several moments and his eyes began to swim with moisture.

"Mr. Lucas?"

"What?" He blinked, shaking off the stare he had been holding. "I'm sorry, David. It's rather beautiful in this light," he raised a pointed finger in direction of the window, "I see it all the time, but on certain days . . ."

And then he was lost again, gazing upon the rainbows as if they were new to him. David looked at the window. It was beautiful, brilliantly lit with sunshine, but was not, in David's opinion, worth the tears that now streamed down Lucas' face.

"Are you alright?"

"Yes." The consumption left Lucas' eyes and the look of calm contemptuous coolness returned. "I brought it here, you know," he said lifting his water glass to his thin lips. "Everyone told me I couldn't, everyone told me I couldn't do lots of things . . . what the bugger do they know, anyway." He laughed, looked up once more with prideful satisfaction, and then got up from the table. "What do you think, Davey, time for the big room?"

"Please don't call me that."

"Oh, bit of a sensitive spot, eh? Well then, I shall reserve it for punishment. Come along, we haven't got all day."

The Lucas estate was large and contained fifteen bedrooms, twenty baths, a master suite, a billiard room, library, office, outdoor pool, and a private studio that occupied the entire west wing of the house. The studio itself appeared to David more as a green house than a place to make music. It was completely constructed of glass. The floor was interchangeable to accommodate acoustics and the ceiling was broken into four segments that could be opened to the sky in good weather.

"I've never seen anything like it," he said, gazing upward at the glass ceiling. "Must have cost-"

"A bloody fortune, yes, yes indeed, but completely worth it, lad. The first record alone paid for the construction of the house and half of the equipment. But that's not why I built it."

"No?"

"No. Don't be such an ass. I built it because *I* wanted it. I already had the money when I came up here. Thirty years of music, David, not a bad living."

"It's overwhelming. How do you keep the trees from growing over it?" David couldn't help but notice the tall pines around the studio, yet not a single needle hung over the transparent glass.

"I don't. If you look you'll see that none of the trees grow beside the house. Drake doesn't even trim them."

"He's your gardener as well?"

"Hardly. There are a few patches of grass that he tends to, but the roses belong to Emily. They're her hobby."

"The little girl?"

"Yes little, but not young. She was my sister's, but came to me after my sister and her husband died in the Columbia last year."

"That's shitty luck." David shook his head.

"Yes, truly, but I think she's happy here with me. A small autism makes public schools impossible, so she studies with Drake three hours a day and reads to me in the evenings. I didn't know flowers could grow up here, but she knew that they would. I come out of the kitchen one morning and where is she? Sitting among rows of roses in the backyard, as if they had always been there. He won't admit to it, but I know Drake went into town to get them for her. He spoils her more than I would like. Enabling the disabled I say. Not the proper way, not in my mind. Pay her no attention, though, Masterson, she has her own eccentricities."

"I'm sure she's very sweet." No, David knew she was. That face, those perfected braids hanging against the cotton background of her dress. Beautiful. Innocent and small in her uncle's gigantic surroundings.

"She is stubborn, but we have an understanding. Let me show you my book, it has every song I've done up here."

"How old is she?"

"She's seven. It's over here." Lucas seemed annoyed at being passed over as the center of attention.

"She doesn't have any brothers or sisters?"

"No. She's an only child. Now, as you can see," he said holding a blue binder with laminated papers in it.

"How severe is her au-"

"Look, David," he slammed the binder shut in between his long bony fingers. "She is no concern of yours. You are up here to help me and if I feel at any time that your work or focus is not where it should be then I'm sure a return flight to California can be arranged." His eyes narrowed and peered into David's face. "Me. Not her. Clear?"

"Yes, Mr. Lucas."

"Right. Better pull out your paper and pen then, mate."

They walked through the studio at a brisk pace, Lucas occasionally pointing out his newest additions and never failing to recite their cost or the length of their construction. David was used to this. He had realized early on that the wealthy often found validation in material possessions. A mink coat that erased a miscarriage. A lavish sports car that overrode a messy divorce. And more often than not, a house that would never fall to the monsters of poverty, abuse, or the horrors of a bad childhood.

The house told it all. Brick walls that protected, several rooms to claim sanctuary, and a large iron gate, impenetrable to even the strongest of the modern world's will. Yup, it was obvious to David that Lucas knew of such sufferings and had built this house to protect himself from them. From the inside it felt tight, almost waterproof, as if locked up. On the outside it looked solid, unyielding, not welcoming, but condemning, its cold tall walls reaching high among the pines, looking down on him. This house, like Lucas, did not want people and David felt unwelcomed by everything - by everything except the red roses.

"This will be your room," Lucas said as he opened one of the several doors down one of the house's many dark hallways. "I had Drake change the sheets for you and there are fresh linens in the toilet."

David entered the medium sized room and looked around. *Thank god it has a big window,* he thought, *this house is a little too closed for me.* There was an antique canopy bed raised high enough off the ground so as to require a stepping stool to climb into it. Beneath the window was a cherry wood desk, chair and dresser. On the far side of the room was a fireplace fronted by a high backed smoking chair and ottoman. The room had something the rest of the house lacked; a woman's touch.

"I love it." David said, extending his hand to his host.

"Good," Lucas replied, shaking the offered limb. "I knew you would. Feminine detail and all. Must be the mama's boy in you."

David shot him a narrow look and scoffed. He wouldn't let Lucas ruin the moment for him. He liked this room and was looking forward to spending some time in it. Alone. No Lucas, no phone, just him and his laptop.

"Well then, I'll leave you to it." Lucas turned towards

the door. "David?"

"Yes, Mr. Lucas?"

"Emily is a very special little girl, but she is also very curious. I will try and dissuade her from your quarters, but I'm not making any promises . . . she may pop in…"

"Of course, no problem."

"Thank you. Enjoy."

CHAPTER SIX

*J*ared Lucas spent most of his afternoons and early evenings in his studio working. He told David that it was only because of Emily and Drake that he locked the double doors to the studio, a testament to his refusal to perform for anyone. It was now, back in front of the den's fireplace, that David sensed his host finally begin to relax. David had spent the remainder of the day in his room, giving Lucas a little bit of the isolated privacy David seemed to penetrate. When Drake knocked on his door at 6:30 for dinner, David was refreshed and ready to be in the presence of his host again. Lucas must have felt similarly because he greeted David with a wide pointed smile. They had dined and retreated to the den for drinks. David had elected for a glass of wine; after all, he was working, but caved in to a whiskey sour at Lucas' nagging. The silver cigarette box sat open in front of them on a glass table, its contents already beginning to dwindle after only an hour. Lucas sat in a high-backed leather chair with his feet rested upon a dark red ottoman. In his left hand a black cigarette burned and in his hanging right, drooped over the side of the chair, a tumbler glass weighted with gin-soaked ice hovered above the carpet. The drinks were beginning to add up.

"My wife was an alcoholic," he began, bringing the almost empty glass to his lips. "She used to drink Bloody Marys in the morning, Long Island Iced Teas in the afternoon, and Whiskey Sours in the evenings."

David thought Lucas' eyes were watering from the booze, but then realized it was tears.

"We used to go down to the beach in the middle of the night and make love on the shore . . . She was all I ever wanted." He looked at David and cleared his throat. "When she finally got sober, she realized what a son of a bitch I was and divorced me shortly then after."

"Did she drink before you got married?"

"No, she partied – that was no secret, so did I. We met at the opening of a restaurant, she ordered whiskey and I . . . ordered a coke." He grinned, the laughter slowly rising out of his throat, out into the open where it grew and seemed to burst. David joined in, partially spilling his own drink. "She knew everything about me," he continued. "She knew, and she loved me anyway."

He polished off his drink and got up to refill. His walk looked to David like that of a cowboy's in an old spaghetti western, half stagger, half strut, as if to say, 'c'mon over and we'll have one 'fore we go.'

"Whatta 'bout you, tiger. Ready for a new one?"

David chuckled as he made his way to the bar. "You know, Jared, generally I'm not supposed to drink when I'm workin'."

"Pish, young son. Enjoy yourself. Life is shorter than you know. Why waste?"

"Good point." David agreed. But anything could have been a good idea, his mind said. *No bad ideas here, son, just bring the hooch. Just watch yourself, you don't know him. Remember that. And what we do know isn't good. Steady.*

"...so then I said to the bartender, slippery nipples all around!" he burst into a drunken laughter and collapsed into his chair.

David grabbed his drink and returned to his chair.

"Have you ever been married, Mr. Mazzzterzon?" Lucas asked, dragging David's last name into one long slurred syllable.

"No, Christ no."

"Oh, 'Christ no', he says. Doesn't sound good," he grinned allowing the firelight to shine off a row of teeth. "What happen, break your heart?"

"Hardly. They're all the same anyway." David didn't

know why he said it. He had always thought the least of guys who couldn't chalk up to losing a girl, but Lucas made him nervous, even now, amongst the booze. *Especially amongst the booze.* "We just didn't make it."

"Oh, really. Funny, I got the feeling there might have been someone else."

Their eyes faced off, Lucas' knowing and manipulating, and David's resisting and confused. David broke his stare and took a swig of his drink.

"She didn't love me anymore." He felt himself start into it and couldn't stop the motion. "I was trying to write a book. We had been together for three years and I hadn't worked in six months. My dad had died and left me a little money, so I quit my part-time teaching job and went home to write my novel. Only problem was, I couldn't write. I tried, my aunt is a novelist, but... I just couldn't do it. So, instead I lay on the couch all day, gained twenty pounds, and proceeded to make both our lives shit. My best friend, Brian, would come over, barbeque, hang out, ya know. They both tried, tried to get me to do, well anything, really, but I wouldn't. All I could do was, nothing."

Lucas sat far back in his chair, appearing to envelop the words as they came out.

"After a few months I started noticing a decrease in their attempts. Pretty soon they stopped asking me to go with them to wherever. It just stopped."

He drummed his nails on his chair's arm feeling past tension wear down his buzz.

"When they told me, it finally dawned on me, they had been dating because I wouldn't get up off the fucking couch. I mean, it was my fault they ended up together all the time. Ironic, isn't it?"

"I dunno about that, but it certainly is rubbish."

Lucas looked into the fire and nursed his juniper juice occasionally letting a few drops drip down his chin without recognition.

"You have a really great setup here. Very comfortable."

"Yes, well, I'm not sure it's all worth it."

"What? You crazy? Most guys would give their left nut to have all this."

"Right, but there's always a position to be held and I . . . don't want it anymore."

"What? Oh please, old man," the liquor was catching up to him, "you can always come back to it. Lots of musicians retire and then come back. Believe me there is nothing more self-stroking than a comeback. Fans eat it up."

Lucas' head tilted to one side and his intense eyes stared at David. "Why do you do that?" he asked.

David thought he looked as sober as a judge. A judge who was judging him. "Do what?"

"Bugger everyone who is a fan of anything? Why is that so bad? Pompous ass."

"Hey, I'm just saying that, that, those who feel passionate about-"

"That those ass-licking freaks are just a bunch of wankers who will eat whatever I give them? Well fuck you, Davey. They have given everything, year after year, even now while I hide out here. What have you ever given? Nothing!" he snapped. "Right, time for bed then."

Lucas rose from his chair and began to walk out of the room. David stared into the fire feeling the heat shrink-wrap his eyeballs.

"And just so's you know, Mr. Wolf," Lucas said, standing in the den's doorway, "I wasn't talking about the music."

CHAPTER SEVEN

*D*avid sat by the fire for another hour and once the room stopped spinning he decided to go to bed. He managed to get out of his clothes and fell face first onto the cool linen. His feet hung off the bed positioning the rest of his body at an angle. He groped for a pillow and brought it down to his head. A short time later he passed out.

He was in a tree-riddled area again, but this time it was pine trees in lieu of the previous weeping willows. He was sitting on a log, his clothes damp from what looked like a late day mist. Afternoon was his guess, but the light gave no indication. A heavy fog hung evenly in the air and twenty feet beyond David's vision stood nothing but grayness. He stood, looking down at the boots, jeans, and fleece he was wearing. He was filthy. Pine needles clung to the soft fabric and he brushed them off.

"Boy."

He looked up and saw a small figure carrying a bag.

"From the plane, right?" he guessed.

"Yes, but I knew you long before dat." She smiled. "How's your head?"

"Fine. Why?"

"Well, ya had a bit of a fall, but Mama Legna pick ya back up agin."

She laughed and walked closer to him. She was short and petite and had to reach quite a bit to place her cool palm on his cheek.

"Pr'haps we walk now, David. What do ya say?"

"Alright."

They began to walk through the fog, which seemed to condense around them with every step.

"Justa bit further," she said, her feet shuffling more than walking. "Here," she said stopping.

"Here, what?" David asked.
"Here we are safe, for da time bein'."
"I don't understand."
"I know. In dreams it always seem dat way, but you will and Mama Legna is goin' to help you."

She stood across from him now, her carpetbag at her feet. She grabbed both of his hands and held them out in the open space between her and him.

"Are you listen', David?"
"Yes."
"Because I won't always be able to come to ya."
"Yes. I'm listening."
"You cannot run, my boy."

His spine began to quiver.

"You cannot run even if you want to. He will hold you and t'hers no gettin' roun' dat."

"What do I do?"

She held up her hand, indicating him to be quiet.

"Yes, here he comes. You must go now. I will try for you agin soon."

She let go of his hands and began to back away.

"No! Wait! Mama! What do I do?" he hollered after her.

"I will send others, boy."

And then she was gone. David stood in the fog-ridden clearing and listened. She was right, someone was coming. Consistent footfalls, even, and heavy. David closed his eyes attempting to hear better, but the sounds could be coming from any direction and he couldn't see. He couldn't see through this fucking fog. Then his feet were pulled out from under him. He was dragged from his previous spot, face down through the needles. He went over a log and when he came back down he was lying on the floor in his bedroom. He stood up quickly and scanned the room. He was alone. The warm fall sun was shining through his window onto his feet. He backed up against the bed and felt something poke his upper thigh. He reached into his boxers and removed a green pine needle.

"Does your room not suit you, young David?"
"What?"
David was at breakfast, but his mind was still in the woods. He barely even noticed when Lucas spoke.
"You look as though you didn't sleep. No worries, I hope."
"Ah, no," he forced a smile. "No worries, Mr. Lucas."
"Good. I was thinking, perhaps, maybe a walk today. The best trails in the world are here on Hood and most of them in my backyard. There are some hiking boots I had Drake place in your closet,"
"I brought my own, thanks."
"Really? A city chap with hiking kegs? Huh, imagine that."
Silence.
"Actually, I love to hike. Took a trip not far from here a couple years ago with a friend."
"Here, in Oregon? When was this?" Lucas asked, leaning closer toward David.
"About two years. Yeah, two years this past summer. We were up past the falls, you know just beyond Bridal Veil?"
Lucas indicated that he did know.
"And we got lost. After three days they had every cop within fifty miles looking for us."
"Someone noticed you were gone?'
"Yeah, a manager at the hotel where we were staying. Said he saw our gear, saw that there wasn't a tent or sleeping bag, just water bottles. Day trip kind of stuff. When we didn't show on our check out day they entered our room, saw that we had left all of our clothes, and realized that we might be in trouble."
He scoffed at the last line because trouble hadn't been the least of it.
"Did your friend get hurt?"
Boy, he doesn't miss a beat does he?
"Yes. Not pain so much as sick. Pneumonia. The

first night out it rained and we didn't have anything with us, just clothes, so we got wet. I was fine, but Brian had asthma and when the morning frost came he started coughing. They said later that he had been getting sick prior to our trip, but he never said anything so I didn't know."

Why are you telling him this? David's mind asked. *So many trips and this is the one you pick? Nice.*

David forced his thoughts quiet and stood up.

"I'll go grab'em. Meet you outside."

He didn't wait for Lucas to respond, but instead shot his gaze to the floor and quickly exited the kitchen.

The morning was cool with the late fall's warmth still clinging beneath it. The sun breaks gave the Lucas estate a much gentler appearance and David began to shake his dream. Lucas exited the house wearing jeans, a black sweatshirt, and Timberlands that made his feet look like the largest parts of his whole body.

"Why don't we take this route," he said, pointing to a path just beyond the carport. "There's a shed at the end of it just in case we get caught in a downpour."

"Should we take umbrellas?" David asked, glancing up at the sky.

"Oregonians don't use umbrellas, Mr. Wolf."

"Really? Not even to protect their granola?"

"Watch it, smartass."

They climbed a small summit that ran east of the house and gave way to a cliff. David hugged the mountain wall that stood tall and enormous on one side of the trail. He had never been fond of heights and if he had known this would be part of the hike he would have told Lucas to knock himself out and that David would see him at lunch. But, what could be done now? Nothing; so David just inched along trying to think about his new big office.

"How's it going back there?" Lucas hollered. "Still in one piece?"

"Oh yeah," David replied, puffing. "Slow as she goes."

Lucas laughed and turned to face David. He had the wall on his right and about two feet to his left the trail dropped off into what seemed to David an endless valley.

"Height trouble, young David?"

"Yeah. I guess Everest will have to wait."

Lucas laughed.

"Yes, well, the good news is that you won't feel a thing. Just a few moments of flight and then nothing."

"Yeah, nothin' but a thud and a stain," David said, still clinging to the wall.

"I thought you said you hiked?"

"I do, but normally there's other trees around and it's more up than across."

"Hardly hiking, city boy."

"Funny, I didn't know London had a lot of trails."

Lucas' eyes narrowed and David felt sure he had crossed the line. "I was born and raised in London, but I traveled a great deal and have hiked better trails than those of your pathetic Big Bear."

"Hey now, no reason to insult the southern mountains."

"Perhaps it is the best you Californians can do."

"We try."

David wanted this conversation to be over, but Lucas continued.

"Always think you have everything. Beaches, deserts, mountains, but the truth is that none of it's genuine. Travel one hour outside of L.A. to visit the mountains? Please. Not even worth having."

David could not think of anything polite to say so he said nothing. He simply stared back at Lucas until he turned and continued walking up the trail.

A short time later the path began to wind upward and they soon found themselves standing in front of a small cabin. Lucas walked up the steps and opened the door without hesitation. David was not surprised to find that the door was unlocked. He thought that they were still on Lucas' property and that Lucas was surely the only person to visit such a location. The inside was mostly empty with the exception of a table, chairs, and sofa. Lucas walked over to a small ice box and pulled out two Coca Colas.

"That must be pretty old," David said, pointing to the box. "Looks like its straight from the 60's."

"I prefer the ones that open from the top," he said, lifting the lid and then letting it drop. "I can store twice as much pop."

"You mean soda?"

"Whatever."

He handed the cola to David and motioned him to take a seat at the table.

"Let's continue our interview, shall we?"

"Yes," David reached into his pocket for his notepad, "that would be great."

He cleared his throat, simultaneously flipping pages of the notepad over and over before finally stopping on a blank one.

"Why did you decide to come up to Mt. Hood?"

"I needed a break."

Lucas looked at David with finality and David motioned for more.

"Not enough? Well, the last record had done exceedingly well and I was receiving a great deal of attention, most of it unwanted."

David had been scribbling madly and paused for a brief moment to look at Lucas.

"Unwanted?"

"Yes. Two weeks before I came up here my sister was kidnapped and held hostage for a ransom. I of course paid it and they returned her to me frightened, but otherwise unharmed."

"I don't remember hearing about that."

"No, I kept it out of the papers."

"But you feel safe talking about it now?"

"Yes, well Lilly has been dead for some time now. That is how I got Emily."

"Do you want to talk about her?"

"No."

David shifted gears.

"So why no outside contact?"

"At first there was and I had people calling day and night. Even had a few trespassers, so I decide to cut off from the world."

"Don't you miss it?"

"No."

"What about your band mates? Your fans? Family? Friends?"

"I didn't leave anybody who wasn't worth leaving." Lucas snapped. "Lilly was the last of them and when she went and Emily came here, I didn't have any reason to keep any ties."

"What about producers? Record labels? You still put music out, how does that work?

"I do all the music myself, track by track. Every instrument, every chord is mine. I then email them to my label and my producers, upon which they give their approval and put it onto a disk. I send them four tracks out of twelve and when they send me a check, I send them the other eight."

"You never go into town?"

"On the record, no. But you David, probably know better. Downtown is hard to stay away from."

David nodded. That big office was definitely his.

"What about women?"

"What about women."

"A man has needs. Do you have any visitors?"

"Ha! Yes, several, day in and day out, prostitutes frolicking around the grounds, their lace teddies occasionally snagging on a branch or tree limb! Ha! You can't be serious."

"So?"

Lucas sighed with irritation.

"I am an old man. I have lived fifty-three years, forty-eight of which were engrossed by females. I'm done."

"That's slightly early, don't you think?"

"P'rhaps." He crossed his arms and sighed. "We'll come back to that, but in the meantime let the record show that I have had a long run with women and deserve a break."

"Fair enough."

"Quite."

"So, you don't think you'll get married again?"

"Sadly, no. I enjoyed being married, but that period is definitely over."

"Did your ex remarry?"

"Yeah, some asshole, owns a ranch in Cristobel, Texas. They moved around quite a bit, but somehow always wind up there."

"Have you dated anyone since?"

"No."

"Are you lying?" David felt the comfort of his notepad in his hand and had slowly settled into his interview routine without noticing; light questions, heavy question, heavier questions, stupid question, and so on.

Lucas smirked, squinted his eyes at the ceiling and then looked at David.

"I wouldn't say I've dated, but I would say that I have been seeing someone."

"Does she live here?"

"No, but she visits frequently."

"When was the last time she was here?"

"Last night."

David stopped his writing and raised his head.

"Last night?"

"Yes. After I left you by the fire."

"I didn't hear anyone."

"Well, you were quite drunk. When I checked on you a while later you were face down on your bed, snoring," he chuckled.

"Oh. She drove in that late?"

"Don't worry about it, Masterson. Yes, I'm seeing someone, no she doesn't live here, and yes she was at the house last night, the end." Lucas seemed irritated. "She comes and goes."

"How do you know when she's coming?"

"I just know, now can we move on to something else!"

"Sure." David blinked and refocused on his questions. "Do you ever plan to return to the outside world?"

"Yes."

"Really? When?"

"I'm actually preparing to be in London next month."

"So soon?" David was surprised. "How do you plan to do it? The public's bound to notice."

"Well, I'm not going as Jared Lucas. Of course not."

"Who, uh, are you going as?"

"Someone else."

They sat for a moment, David's eyes bugging out of his head, Lucas' level and slightly hooded. When he finally spoke David couldn't help but jump.

"Think we should head back, young David. Getting late."

CHAPTER EIGHT

The hike back to Lucas's house seemed to span across centuries. David felt exposed by the silence in which they walked, as if his footsteps themselves offended the quiet. Lucas said nothing, no witty comments about the slope to their left, no mocking grins at David's discomfort, just silence. After the drastic ups and downs of their previous conversations, David might have thought a verbal rest to be a relief, but instead found it more unnerving than the communication minefield he was wandering through.

They reached the front steps of the house and began to unlace their mud-covered boots. Lucas finished first and opened the front door.

"How about a siesta, young David? I'm really a bit tired and would appreciate a nap. Work for you?"

"Certainly, Mr. Lucas. I can entertain myself."

Lucas nodded and headed into the house, leaving the door open behind him.

David sat quietly on the brick steps for a few moments, trying to piece together what Lucas had said. A trip to London? He snapped his head up when a shadow fell over him.

"Did you enjoy your walk, Mr. Masterson?" Drake stood above him, smiling. "Yeah. Made it all the way to the shack. Didn't plummet to my death once."

Drake laughed. "He does like to make people uncomfortable, that's for sure. Most rich people do. I don't know. Seems to me that financial security might make one more patient, sympathetic. No, Mr. Lucas is definitely different."

"What kind of different?"

"You know, the competitive kind. Suspicious, territorial. And it has nothing to do with money, I'll tell you that." He took his hands out of his pockets and slowly lowered himself onto the step next to David. "Believe me there is nothing more entertaining for him than someone who doesn't see him coming."

"Like me?"

"Like you."

"I can handle him."

"Oh really? I'm not so sure. He's tough, you know."

"Well yeah, he's an icon. Can't be weak and make it that far." David looked at Drake who was turned sideways, staring directly at him.

"That's not what I'm talking about." His eyes shifted back and forth, scanning David's face.

"What?"

"Is there something you want to ask me about Mr. Lucas, David?" he asked, his eyes focusing harder and harder on David's features.

"How is he going to London?"

David thought that was the right question, but when Drake shook his head and stood up, he knew it wasn't.

"I'm sorry Mr. Masterson, you'll have to ask him about that." As he walked into the house, Drake turned around to look at the young man sitting with his back to him. He did not look the way he thought he would. So young, but strong, unusually strong at his center. Drake closed the door behind him and entered the den where he found Lucas sitting in his high backed chair.

"What do you think you are doing, old man?"

"My job, Lucas."

"You can tell him nothing!" Lucas snapped, his fingers sprawled angrily over each arm of the chair. "I have my time and it is to be uninterrupted by you!"

"He will not need me. Your vanity has betrayed you. Instead of choosing a weak soul to overpower, you have chosen a strong one."

"A strong one that I will maintain!"

"If, if you can get him. That's the problem with the

pure ones, they don't give over that easily. Of course, I don't need to tell you that."

"Right! My choice, Drake, my choice, no one else's."

"And what do you have to show for it? Hmmm? Locked away up here, your soul more confined than ever. Why not call it quits?"

Lucas scoffed, "Are you mad? Give up? Now? After all this? Why should I?"

"Because, he is going to be the end of it."

"You don't know that!"

"Yes I do. He will not fall. He is awake."

"No, I don't think so." His eyes smiled, sharing his demeanor. "He is slowly drowning in his own fear. And those silly dreams, why, he might just die in his sleep and then I would be rid of all this nonsense."

"We will protect him."

"Like the one before me?" Lucas' eyebrows lifted, awaiting an answer, but Drake said nothing. "Right, that one didn't work out either. Interesting. Seems to me your side is losing. And Masterson? He is no obstacle to me. You will see."

Drake's posture lowered and he shifted his weight.

"It is not for you to make me see, Jared." His voice was firm and he felt it make its way across the room to his competitor. "You weren't strong enough, he is, as are we, and this will be the end of those ways."

"Not if they can help it, angel. Not if I can."

When David was a young boy he often wondered why bad things happened to good people and why good things happened to bad people. Now, as an adult he had lost his curiosity, completely convinced that one's moral place in the world had nothing to do with temperamental luck. He was sure he was a good man, not without flaw, but sincerely good all the same and as such was able to identify those men who were not good. And Jared Lucas most certainly was not a good man. David wasn't sure exactly what it was, wasn't sure if it was any one thing in particular, but he knew it. The passing hours in the Lucas house amplified his suspicion and by evening he began to feel the need to make contact with the outside world.

"Hey Martin, it's David."

"David, how's it going?"

"Fine, good, um, damn good. I have some great notes."

"Uh-huh, and what about Lucas?"

"Edgy. Fantastic, really. He's kinda strange though, boss."

"Is he giving you problems?"

"Oh no, he's just odd, you know. I mean, frankly I don't know what I'm doing here. He doesn't really wanna talk about anything."

"Not anything? What about your notes?"

"Well yeah, I have some stuff, but nothing really great, but there's this little girl,"

"Dave, nobody has had an interview with the guy in years. No matter what we print, it will sell."

"Yeah, I know that but..."

"What about a little girl?"

"Oh, he has his niece living up here with him, it's his sister's kid, she's dead now, but the little girl is autistic."

"Really, no shit?"

"I know, right, and get this, he has a butler named Drake."

"I thought he didn't employ a staff."

"I know, that's what I thought, but he's here and I think him and the little girl...well, that's the story, I'm positive that's it."

"What's her name?"

"Emily. She's seven, I think, but listen, he doesn't like talking about her, I mean, at all, so don't count on anything for sure in that department, okay?"

"Whatever, asshole. Do what you can."

"Alright. I'll call you tomorrow."

David pressed the END button on his phone and felt

his comfort disappear with the electronic light. The room was quiet, but his mind spoke in rapid succession. *Going as someone else . . . yes, she was here last night . . .* He decided to take a nap. He didn't feel like writing. The afternoon had been exhausting and his body ached from the unwavering intensity that Lucas seemed to trigger in him. His room had already begun to grow dark despite the early hours. *Daylight is short in these parts.* He slipped off his socks and shirt, creating a soft, small cluster on the floor by his bed. The comforter was gentle to his sighing muscles and he soon felt the room's darkness intensify.

The sensation started at his feet and slowly crept up to his ankles and calves. It felt to David like cool, delicate fingers dancing lightly along his skin. His eyes were closed, but through his lids he could see an approaching light filling his room. Up past his knee and onto the tops of both thighs fluttered the fingers, awakening his skin inch by inch. His body mildly flexed as the fingers brought their slight chill across his stomach, onto his chest, and up over his chin to his forehead. There a pressure rested. He opened his eyelids, half expecting the morning sun to be glaring through his window, but instead found darkness, and sitting in that darkness, at the foot of his bed was a woman.

"Hello, David."

Her voice was soft and low, delicate in tone and caressing in pitch. Her hair was long and curly and draped over her shoulders and down her chest, its dark color contrasting with the white nightgown she wore. Her face was young and simple with bright eyes and a pleasant mouth.

"Hi." He managed as he propped himself up against the bed's headboard.

"It's very peaceful in here," she said, gazing around the room. "I don't think I've ever actually been in here before."

"This house is rather large," David responded, not knowing exactly what to say.

"Yes, it is. Jared built it, you know. This house is everything for him."

She was looking at him now and he felt himself staring at her, taking in her beauty and registering her presence. It was very strong. He waited a moment longer, but felt too awkward to contain himself.

"Who are you?"

"I'm Rebecca." She watched him for recognition and saw none. "Didn't Mama tell you I was coming?"

"Mama? The old woman, you mean?"

She laughed, "yes, she is quite old, but also very important. She told you she would send others, remember?"

He did remember. As a matter of fact he remembered everything about Mama Legna, as if she were real to him and not part of a dream.

"She isn't real, I mean, on the plane I saw her, but we didn't..."

"I assure you she is. Just like me."

"Yeah, but I can see you. I'm not asleep now,"

"Do you have such little faith in your mind? Mama is a real being. She comes to you in dreams because it is easier for you."

"Easier? How?"

"She gave you a message didn't she?"

David's heart slowed as if life was falling out of it. "She told me. . ."

"That you couldn't run."

David's palms were streaming with sweat and he could feel his pulse rush below their surface.

"That is what she said, isn't it, David?"

"Yes."

"Well, there is only one thing to do if you can't run," she was sliding off the bed, her bare feet meeting the floor with quiet impact.

"What's that?" he asked.

"Stay and fight, of course."

"Fight against what? What is this all about?" His face grew hot with frustration. "What the hell is going on? Why are you in my room? Who is Mama Legna and why does she keep following me?"

"You don't know?"

"No!"

"Jared, of course. He's a fallen star. He traded his soul for thirty years of perfection on earth and now his time is up. If he doesn't trade with a new soul by the end of harvest he will cease to exist and the people who gave him this life will be denied their ways here."

David stared at the feminine statue in bewilderment. He wanted to scoff at her, to tell her that he stopped doing drugs in high school and that he wasn't fond of practical jokes. But his mind spoke again and with its acknowledgement came belief. *She's telling the truth. He is a bad man and now you know why.*

"Oh shit." David felt his face tighten. "How long has this been going on?"

"Centuries. Mankind has been the subject of temptation since time began, but a while back an angel realized how strong man's greed could be. So, he approached a man, offered him thirty years of wealth, success, and unparalleled worship in turn for an opportunity to collect his soul. If an angel collects a soul he can return to earth as a mortal thus ending his eternity of guardianship. Man agreed and the result was the establishment of monarchy and the birth of slavery. Since then earth has been a battleground, good and its loyal on one side and evil and its followers on the other."

"Wait, evil? So, all the murderers, thieves, and con artists of the world aren't human?"

"Not even close." She smiled and it looked like pride to him. "They are the angels who have escaped their guardianship, but still retain a sense of immortality and righteousness, which is now controlled by human emotions that they have never had before. Often the result is insanity, excessive cruelty . . . death. Humans naturally reject such atrocities."

"And then what happens? Can they actually die?"

"Yes. Human form is very fragile. When their soul leaves the body they are returned to the gates where they await judgment, just as all humans do. The majority are returned into guardianship, but occasionally one is let through."

"Really? Let into heaven?"

She blinked and looked away, "It happens."

"So corrupt angels and good angels, fallen stars? Which one are you?"

"Surely you know. The others are... let's just say they don't look like Jared."

"Are they going to come find me, too?"

"They can't, not here and not while you're awake," she walked over to where he was lying and placed her hand over his. "But they can find you in your sleep. That is where we are most vulnerable. Your mind is open to all universal entities and horrors. We are trying to protect you until you can face Jared and end the cycle, but should you find yourself alone in a dream, call for me and I will come. I must go now."

She left his side and walked over to the window's edge, opened the glass, and sighed. And then she was gone. David sat staring at the window. Somewhere in the south the tide was coming in. Beachgoers were packing up children in multicolored bathing suits and commenting to each other that the temperature was already dropping. Their tanned skin would soon be covered in O'Neil sweatshirts and Cargo pants. Bonfires would take light and hot dogs would emerge from ice chests sunk deep in the sand like boulders. Families would play Frisbee, while couples drank wine and the sun fell into the beautiful Pacific. They were safe there, near his home, among the sand and in a place of trees with no leaves. They were where he should have been.

"Help. Oh god I need help." His voice was clear and

cut through the silence like shears. Why had he come?

The trees were thicker this time, their height closing off the sky as their arms stretched in every direction. David felt the damp coolness surround his body and knew his dreaming was real. He also knew he wasn't alone.

"Mama?"

A childish giggle came from behind a tree and before David could turn, the strawberry blonde haired girl was standing in front of him.

"Hi," she said walking closer to him.

"What are you doing here?" David asked, his body tensing as the memory of her scent filled his head.

"You tell me, champ. It's your dream."

"Kind of a long way from the airport."

"Yeah, well, we don't have to be here." She smiled.

"We don't?"

"Course not." She placed her hand over his eyes while the other found its way across his shoulders, pulling him close to her. She removed her hand and David opened his eyes to see that they were back in his apartment in California, lying on his weathered queen bed covered in his only pair of sheets.

"Is this real?" he asked not really caring.

"It can be. It can be whatever you want."

Her hand floated across the bare skin of his chest and he could feel her lips tracing its steps. There had been no one since Melissa and he had missed it, missed the sensation of being touched. Her hair draped over his stomach and his mind registered her naked flesh pressed against him, feeling him and suddenly surrounding him. He arched off the bed, rising despite her weight on top of him. She was warm and generous, moving to his pleasure and increasing his every sensation. His body responded with a furious climax and he fell, almost back into himself, onto his pillow. Above him he saw her smile, her face lit in satisfaction, and pride. Her eyes were so green…

A knock on his door woke David and he instinctively reached for the sheets to cover himself, but then realized his jeans were, as they had been before his nap, securely on his body. He wiped his sweaty forehead and smoothed his hair. The knock came again and David rushed to the door. He opened it to find Drake holding a towel and a pair of board shorts.

"Mr. Lucas has requested that you join him in the Jacuzzi for cocktails before dinner."

"Sounds great," his voiced wavered a bit and he felt as if he were an adolescent again being interrupted by his parents at an aroused moment.

"Very good. What can I get for you? Gin?"

"Sure. Gin is fine."

"Okay, Mr. Lucas is having a Tom Collins, but I think I'll make you a gin and tonic; you look like you could use a refresher."

"Yes, um, right, thanks, 'preciate it."

"Sure. Better hustle, Mr. Masterson. Mr. Lucas isn't a patient man."

CHAPTER NINE

*D*avid stepped through two French doors that led out onto an open deck where a hot tub sat, its rising steam accenting the cold night air. Through that curtain of heat David could see Lucas blowing puffs of smoke, his body hidden by the cavernous pond of water in which he was seated. David watched him for a moment, seeing his competitor for the first time with clear eyes. He didn't need the story any more. Martin could take his big office and burn it to the ground for all that David cared. He wasn't going to give into this man, fallen star or *whatever the fuck*. This situation was over David's head and he wanted out.

The dream with the strawberry blonde had been real enough and David was sure that he was being slowly penetrated and manipulated into whatever mindset Lucas wanted. They had tapped his loneliness and used it against him, reminding him of what a woman felt like. The feeling every human recognizes as brief completeness. He would have to dissolve that resource or the pressure in his mind, in his body, would quickly rip him apart.

"Evening, Mr. Lucas," he said, shedding his towel onto a chaise, feeling the cold air hit his body like a wave. "Time for a dip?"

"Yes, well, it's hard to deny the scenery."

His arm swept out in a large half circle over his head and David looked to the heavens. Every star seemed to shine brighter than its neighbor.

"It's incredible. I take it that downtown Portland lights have no effect here."

"No, but they are also impressive themselves."

He looked peaceful to David, content with his realization and in no hurry to acknowledge another one. David slid into the Jacuzzi and initially jumped at its temperature.

"Too hot, Masterson?" Lucas mocked, taking another drag off his dark stick.

"Yeah, slightly toasty."

"Don't be a prat, just get in already."

"I'm coming, just need a minute to-"

"Well come on then. No need to wait til it's cold and useless."

"Like you?"

David's anger was rising. He was nobody's puppet, especially not to this guy, but it was stupid. He didn't have room to push Lucas the wrong way, but the words had come out any way and now Lucas stared at him with narrow eyes. The peace was gone.

"Perhaps," Lucas said, crushing his cigarette into a silver tray.

David caught his breath in his chest and eased completely into the water. He raised his hands to press back his hair and felt the heat rise from them like a candle. Lucas had returned to looking upwards and after a few moments David felt his harsh words drift away.

"Did you sleep?" Jared asked, not facing him.

"Yes. My room is great, Mr. Lucas. It is very comfortable and the bed is perfect."

"I'm glad. It is definitely different from the other rooms in the house. It gets the most light and it was the first room to be completely finished when the house was built. Emily plays in there a great deal usually, but when she heard we were to have a guest, she took to the attic as she sometimes does."

"The attic? The house doesn't look like it has one."

"Oh yes. A spare room in the far north wing. I generally store equipment and such there, but she enjoys solitude. It's her hiding place. I don't think she even knows that I know about it."

"Where is she tonight? Will she be eating with us?"

"No. She will be with Drake, of course. She doesn't

enjoy being with me very much. He is more her type of company. Children and old people, you know. Strange bond."

Lucas seemed more disgusted than hurt by Emily's preference and David found it odd to hear him speak of her with such resentment. What type of man resents a child?

"Will she be going with you to England next month?"

"No," he answered, letting the words exit his mouth with a smile trailing softly behind them. "I will be going alone."

"What about your lady friend? Women don't like to be left behind, from what I've gathered."

"And why is that, young David? Tell me, how long was your girl laying it out for your best friend before you finally wised up?"

David sat shell-shocked. He should have seen this coming. Lucas was always one to bite back and David hadn't been ready. His viciousness was so direct, so controlled and David was beginning to see what he should have seen yesterday. Beginning to see what Rebecca had warned him about.

"Longer than I would've liked."

"Obviously. Tell me, did they end up together?"

"Far as I know."

Lucas' words were laced and David began to feel like a freshman whose drink had been spiked.

"Of course they did. Why on earth would a lovely woman, such as your Melissa, with youth, brains and a tight body with a snatch to match want to be with a wanker asshole like you?"

"Could've been worse. I could have drank myself stupid, screwed every back up singer from L.A. to London and impregnated not one, but two of my band mates' wives." The words held between them heavy and present, briefly, until Lucas laughed them into evaporation.

"Yes," he smiled, "there is always that. But as least I would have the sex to show for it."

"I'm not entirely sure any piece is worth that much trouble." David allowed himself a feigned chuckle. He hated these words. These Lucas words that had wormed their way into his mind and out his mouth, but he had to play. Playing was the only way out.

"I don't believe that, young David. I don't believe that at all. You don't strike me as a man careless with the opposite sex."

"Every woman is different. Each has her own, let's say, oddities, but I don't have the patience to discover and dissolve each one. Even the physical proponents have become complicated and I just don't need that."

"So, what? No sex? Ever? Bollocks. No man in his right mind could handle that. No man in his senile mind could handle it."

"I can. Zero sex is a small sacrifice for an eased mind."

"You're insane. Sex is god and no sex is hell. A few people have written on it, asshole."

"That's fine, but for me it works."

Lucas furiously pushed his body away from his seat and stood in the center of the tub, desperately trying to light another cigarette. The black paper caught and he inhaled with tense absorption. He exhaled and dropped his shoulders, securing a posture less aggravated, but David knew his slices were working. He wanted Lucas to squirm. Then perhaps he could leave. He could leave this stupid fucking mountain and go back to a place where the sun and the people shone.

"Let's just say, for a laugh, that you manage to contradict the existence of man and live an entire life without a single fuck on your record. Then what?" His shoulders had crept back up around his ears, making him appear smaller than he was. David countered his posture by lazily draping his arms over the edge of the tub and letting his head rest back onto the wooden deck floor.

"Then nothing," he answered.

"What do you mean nothing? Everybody needs something!"

"I don't. I can find release in other ways. Priests have been doing it for years."

"Priests? You don't look like a fucking priest to me, mate. No, no, you look like a sad little wanker who couldn't get a piece of ass if it was sitting on his fucking lap!"

David wanted to respond, he wanted to tell Lucas that he loved women, loved them inside and out, that the strawberry blonde was tight and warm and wet, but Lucas already knew that. He knew she was and had sent her to confuse David and refresh his memory of what true weakness was. David had given in, had let her, but now he was done.

Lucas stood, smoking cigarette hanging from his lips, arms lanky and long at his sides and nothing but a confused stare filling the air between him and David. His pause lingered until the cigarette finally fell into the bubbling water.

"Oh Christ! See! See what your schoolboy bullshit did? There's goddamn ash all over the bloody place!" He stepped past David, rising out of the tub, the steam flowing off his skin in a dense fog behind his movement's wake. David should have felt satisfaction in Lucas' irritation. He had done what he set out to do, no sex meant no power, but instead of contentment, fear came. It rolled over him and weighted his mind. He realized now that he wasn't pushing Lucas into kicking him out. He was provoking him into making David stay. He acted upon the connection.

"I suppose," he said, stepping out of the tub, skipping three steps to immediately reach the deck's surface. "That we all have an itch that needs to be scratched from time to time. Just some more than others."

Lucas turned to him with a slightly satisfied smirk. The towel he had been drying himself with dropped from one hand to the other, allowing most of it to wallow in a water mark by his feet.

"So you admit your claim to abstinence is complete bollocks and that no man could go without sex?"

"Yeah. I admit it."

"Not even yourself?"

"Yup, not even myself."

Jared tossed him the dampened towel. "I knew you were bluffing." He was so proud at David's admittance. He stood tall with his hands propped upon his hips, his shapely abs and arms flexed in self-satisfaction. Now was as good a time as any.

"Mr. Lucas, I was thinking that perhaps I would leave tomorrow. I have business to take care of in downtown and I won't have enough time if I stay til Sunday."

Lucas thought for a moment. He was taken aback by Masterson's request. They had obviously reached him sooner than Lucas had anticipated. A great deal sooner than the last one.

"'Fraid not, young David. We have quite a few things to discuss, details you see and I have plans for us. It just isn't feasible, but I'm sure Drake would be more than happy to visit Government Camp or Bridal Veil if you need anything. Better shower and dress for dinner. We are having company tonight."

"Who?" David couldn't hide his surprise. He was compromised. He was also losing his battle.

"My lady friend has agreed to join us. Dinner is served at 8:00 PM."

He left and David stood for a moment, feeling the cold darkness around him. He looked to the surrounding trees and wondered how long . . . on foot . . . with food? Jared had said 'no'. He said 'no' because he knew. David's heart sank.

CHAPTER TEN

There were plenty of things David didn't know about Jared Lucas, plenty of things that Mama Legna would have said, that Lucas didn't know about himself. Things that every person, living or dead, carries with them like a darkness. Even those who are aware of the shadows inside their minds struggle under their presence. Mama Legna would have said it was the natural order of things. Mama Legna would have said that all men endure, but even she knew that that wasn't the whole of it. Men don't just endure, they suffer.

David had known his fair share of suffering. He had lost his mother to cancer when he was sixteen, withstood her abusive nature until then and expelled a sigh of gratitude when her body finally gave out. The guilt of this relief had haunted him well into his college years and by the time he graduated with his Masters he was a full blown alcoholic. He could drink in private to fill the void of isolation he himself had created and still pretend by day to be the well rounded individual everyone thought him to be. It went on for years, until Melissa. She had been the answer for him, the reason to stop. She was the only good thing in his life and when she left he could feel his mind reaching for his old ways, wanting to succumb to them and be a ruined man. For truly ruined men, the suffering was over.

He had emerged through the rough patches without backsliding into oblivion, but the edge of the world always seemed within reach should he ever reconsider. Now with his known universe expanding into multiple worlds where angels were in existence and responsible for the rages of mankind, the edge seemed to be the only place left to stand. There were so many questions that needed to be asked, so many answers to be had and finally fulfilled by those who knew the truth behind everything, but David didn't care. All he could think about was escape. He didn't want to know the history of man, the rationale behind separate worlds, or even the presence of a higher power. All he wanted was to be far away from Jared Lucas and off this mountain. This hunger shamed him and all he could feel to do was wait.

The 8:00 hour came more quickly than usual it seemed and David found himself lingering in his room until a minute before. He had hoped for something, anything – Drake, Rebecca or even Mama Legna. Somebody to help him. It had finally occurred to him as he stood in the shower moments before that if he intended to leave prior to his dismissal, he would no doubt be going on foot and in quite a hurry. He had remained there, under the showerhead, frightened and uncertain until its water ran cold. How had this all happened so fast? *This is how it happens*, his mind answered. Could he leave? Why not just get in his truck and head down? *He will find you.* Down the mountain and into Portland. Portland. It sounded so good to his straining mind. People, restaurants, buses, even that rugged little sports bar off the Terwilliger Curves near the college where he lost a game of pool to a tattooed bartender and nearly lost his teeth when he refused to pay up. Cyclists, students, lawyers, hikers, hippies, they all sounded like freedom to him, a return to something warm. There was nothing warm about this mountain. It was no mystery to David why people died up here. He could almost feel them as steady as the stream of cold water that was running across his shoulders.

The water's temperature registered in his mind, but not his body. He stood, motionless, letting it cover him. He wanted it to envelop him. He lowered himself to the floor of the shower, extending his legs behind him, allowing the side of his face to rest in the puddles that gathered there, his body sealing the drain. He lay flat, pressed to the dark tile slightly floating in the shallow lake, arms at his side, engulfed in the peace that seemed to spread over him. The water rose above the field of vision in his right eye and began to climb toward his left. He could feel it sliding gently into his nose, trying to force its way into his lungs. His mouth was slightly agape and he could see the ripples his shallow breathing sent across the water. This could be it for him, he thought. A couple more minutes and the water would be too high for him to breathe. *This is a way out. The truth is, you can leave any time you want to.* David pushed his upper body off the tile with a shudder. Was that his thought? No, he certainly didn't think so. That was someone else. He looked around the shower expecting to see someone, expecting to hear them again. He sat up all the way and pressed his body against the tiled wall away from the shower's stream. What had he almost done? Who was that just now... who was it that just . . . saved him? What had they said? David rose to his feet, turned off the water with a violent shove and raced into his room to get dressed. He wouldn't take his suitcase, no, just a knapsack. If he wanted to make it down the mountain by morning he would have to pack light.

"Darling, you must relax if this is going to work."

Lucas looked at the petite blonde and gave her a look of indignation. "I know what I am doing."

"Really?" she scoffed. "Then why the difficulty? He isn't very quick you know, even Drake knows that." She let her small body slide down onto the silk bedspread, casually lying on her side with one hand propping her head up so that when she spoke she had to look upwards to meet Lucas' eyes. He was standing in front of his dresser, shirt unbuttoned, barefoot, putting on his watch with wild, frustrated fingers.

"Let me help," she said, rising to her knees and reaching for his wrist. Her fingers moved so quickly across the watch's surface and onto its clasp that Lucas barely noticed. He was looking at himself in the mirror, preoccupied by the light behind his eyes. *It's the life light* the angel had told him. *If you don't trade up with another soul, I get it.*

"Don't worry, baby," she was behind him, looking past his shoulder into the mirror. "It will be fine."

"How can I not? He's already convinced. He knows about the dreams."

"But he doesn't know everything. Mama is old and tired, you said so yourself, and she won't be enough anyway, right?"

Lucas looked at the blonde hair, shining eyes, and felt fortified. She had been able to do it, this small, young mind had stolen a soul and kept her own.

"Mama was stronger then, for you, so, how did you-"

"I pushed," her face hardened. "I pushed until my Masterson broke into a thousand pieces," she smirked. "He did it himself, in the end. I didn't even get my hands dirty. Couldn't handle it, like most. Kept expecting someone to save him. They really are sheep, you know. Quite sad."

"What then?" he asked.

"Then, you go back to being as you were, the age you were before the agreement, but with a clean slate and no limitations. I disappeared. People assumed I died. It was easier than I thought," her face looked girlish in its confession. "And you must do the same. He is on the verge of breaking, I know it, darling. Just a little longer."

"And if he doesn't break?"

"Then nothing," their eyes locked. "Literally, Jared . . . nothing."

CHAPTER ELEVEN

Martin Mitchell was a busy man. When he slept, he slept hard, dead to the world, unless a light was on. He could see the brightness through his eyelids and it immediately registered in his mind that Virginia had left the bathroom light on. So many things that spouses do, so many odds and ends that only their mates could identify, complicate the fluidity of a marriage. She was always saying that he was impatient. He thought she was right, but he also thought patience would be a tall order for someone who was denied sleep. She always did this, wash her face, take off her robe, leave it on the floor, sip from a water glass on the nightstand and then proceed to fall asleep without even the slightest difficulty. Bathroom light left on, wife out cold. Martin wondered if it was possible to hate someone that he loved so much, even if only in a very small way.

  He threw back the blankets without opening his eyes, lowered his feet to the floor and slowly stood himself up. His shuffle was more drowsy than aged. He was relatively young at fifty-five and despite his wife's physical distance, had kept himself quite fit. He loved being outside and often hiked the trails behind his house near the sign. They had closed Mulholland to cars, but he was still able to walk up to it on foot.

  The light was on. She had returned her toothbrush to its allotted space in the medicine cabinet, next to his and more importantly, next to the aspirin. He was going to wake up with a migraine in about an hour and a prophylactic shot of the bitter white tablets might buy him some time. He grabbed the bottle and closed the mirrored door. As soon as the metal latch reached home, his eyes met that of another whose reflection replaced his own. Martin dropped the bottle. The creature was dark, ever so dark, with long hair and crystal blue eyes that made Martin feel like crying. The creature spoke, but Martin heard nothing, but his heartbeat in his ears. He slammed his eyes shut only to open them to his own reflection. His brow dripped with sweat and his hands were shaking.

"Nightmare."

He stepped away from the mirror, walking backward towards the door. He turned off the light with a twitching finger and returned to bed. Virginia was sleeping on her left side. Martin slipped into bed and pressed his chest to the back of her nightgown, wrapped his arm around her and tried to find comfort in her presence. He woke several hours later, wanting to roll over, but couldn't bring himself to face the open door of the bathroom. When the alarm went off at five thirty, Martin grabbed his robe from the closet and headed downstairs to shower. Virginia would notice and would surely have a comment for him, but it was worth the hassle.

"Why are you hiding in here?"

Drake looked down at the sandy pigtails and felt an enormous sense of responsibility. She was so beautiful in her little sweater and overalls, playing quietly with her Barbie in this rather dank and unpleasant room. It was odd how the weather always managed to seep into the house this time of year, he thought. Never a crack or a hole to come through, but somehow it always did.

"Busy," she replied, stroking the doll's shiny blonde hair.

"Well now, how about you come on out and get ready for dinner? Your uncle has guests and we should make an appearance, don't you think?" It was obvious that no, she didn't think so. "Emily, time to put the Barbie away. C'mon now." He held out his hand to her and after a moment she rose to her feet and took it, still holding the small figure in her free hand. "Why not leave it, dear? You don't have to pretend around me."

"Better this way," she said.

"You're the boss," he chuckled. God, she amazed him. "What about the others?" He pointed a long, dark finger to the pile of tiny people lying next to a plastic dollhouse. She paused for a moment, staring at the dolls.

"No," she said, "they're fine for now. I only need this one."

CHAPTER TWELVE

The arrangement at dinner was not what David had expected. The dining room was formal enough, but Lucas was dressed casually as was the woman seated to the right of him. They were talking quietly, eyeing each other over wine glasses, exchanging little laughs that David found almost unbearable to listen to.

"Ah, David. Welcome." Lucas greeted David with a handshake and a warm smile, which ironically eased the anxiety growing in David's stomach. "This is my lovely Christine."

The woman stood and reached across the table to offer David her hand. No one had done such a habit of tradition in David's presence since his great grandma was alive. And as if she was there to critique his etiquette, David lightly pecked the beauty's smooth skin. She was quite lovely, a celebrity of some kind. If she was a movie star, he had never seen her before, but he knew that a studio or label was paying hard money to keep her well maintained. There wasn't a single flaw on her exposed skin and David doubted very much that her pink blouse was hiding one. She was virtually perfect.

"Jared tells me that you are writing the first interview with him in quite a long time."

"Quite a long time, dear," Lucas echoed.

"Yes. The first in a couple decades it seems." David thought this conversation was obvious bullshit, polite chatter to soothe his nerves.

"And what angle will you take? The lonesome musician? The brilliant recluse?"

"The flattered prick?" Lucas said, chuckling at his own deprecation.

"I'm not entirely sure." David's lips almost felt as if

they were trembling.

"No lovely, he thinks that I am an egocentric prat, living solely on my arrogance and self indulgent environment. Isn't that right, mate?"

David thought his reply would come out in the form of vomit if he opened his mouth. He mustered a smile on one side of his mouth, trying to conceal the grimace below it. Something wasn't right.

"Hmmmm. Well, we'll just have to see now, won't we." Lucas drank from his wine glass, but never dropped his eyes from David. This is the guy? he thought. This is the guy that's going to change everything? Not a chance. Christine was right and he gave her a small wink.

"David, I wonder if Jared has told you about his *other* hobbies." Her voice seemed to rise with the question, as if the importance of it could be conveyed through pitch.

"Christine, I don't think this is the time." His voice was stern and more recognizable to David now. All that other nonsense, the charm and warmth, anything possibly human was a lie. He was, as he currently was – controlling, intimidating and David thought, maybe, a little scared.

"Come, come darling, it isn't all bad. I'm sure Mr. Masterson would be enlightened by your ability, perhaps even slightly amu-"

"That's enough, Christine." He was gripping the stem of his glass with such intensity that David thought it might break.

"It is not!" she snapped. "A worthy adversary should be advised of all the rules. No need to cheat, Jared."

"Oh, I'm not really one for games," David intervened. "Not much of a competitor either." His voice was steady, but the words fell from his mouth like lead. He was sweating.

"Never mind, David. Jared will go easy on you the first couple of rounds, won't you dear?"

Lucas thought for a moment and then released his

brow from its distraught state. A smile filled his face. "Of course, lovely. Yes, Masterson," he turned towards David and leaned a weighted elbow on the table. "We need to get started, don't you think?"

"What kind of game are we talking about?"

"Certainly not chess, as you can imagine. It's more about instinct, wouldn't you say dear?"

Christine nodded and giggled, "Oh yes, most definitely about . . . intuition."

"The rules are quite simple. First, no outside help. You can't ask Christine or anybody else for aid. Number two, no stopping once the game starts. You stop, I win and I don't like winning by default."

"But he'll happily accept the forfeit anyway," Christine chimed.

"Yes, I will, but do try, mate, all the same. Number three, on foot only. You cannot employ vehicle, flight or otherwise."

"Why would I use a plane?" David questioned.

"No, no, no, not a plane you dumb bugger! Never mind, you'll see what I mean. And lastly, the results are final. You win, then *you* win. If I win, *I* win. No changing minds, no going back. Word of honor and all that. Clear?"

"When do we play?"

"After dinner. It's better to have a bite first. These games can be a bit lengthy."

"Excuse me, Mr. Lucas, but Emily would like to say 'goodnight'." Drake and his small companion entered the dining room. She made her way from Christine, who she kissed on the cheek to Lucas, who hoisted her up onto his lap. Her Barbie hung over the edge of the chair's arm. Lucas held it up to examine it, with Emily's hand still grasping its middle.

"Dearest, you shouldn't carry your dollies around. What if she were to get lost? How sad would you be?"

"I don't lose my dollies," she replied, so matter-of-factly.

"No, you don't." Lucas caressed her hair, almost entranced by its softness and color. How ironic that such a beautiful creature would admire something as common and basic in appearance as a Barbie doll. He realized he had an audience and abruptly kissed her forehead and scooted her off his lap. "Sweetest of dreams, dearest. Drake, good night."

"Good night, Mr. Lucas. Ma'am, sir. Sleep well."

The room sat quiet for a moment, the remaining three sitting around the large table. Lucas gazing beyond the cloth and candles to the window across the room and David struggling with his feeling that refused to subside. *Something*, his mind said. *You know it is something.*

"Well, I should get dinner. Jared, will you help me?"

"Certainly." Lucas rose from the table, but his eyes remained glazed over. No sooner had they left the room then a voice came from the foot of the table. There she sat, small as ever, kind even in her posture.

"Hello, boy."

"Hello. . . Mama?"

"Yes. Rebecca tol' me about your talk."

"Our talk? Is that what she is calling it?" His voice was harsh, but low. He didn't know why, but Lucas finding Mama Legna here, talking to him, seemed like a very bad idea.

"Don't do dat, boy. Don't let 'em shake you. That's how he'll win."

Oh god, David thought, *win. That's how he'll win.* The realization hit him and hurt.

"The game?"

She nodded.

"What is it?"

"Can't say. But I can tell you dat it's extremely important dat you are successful."

"Why? Why me? What am I supposed to do?"

She sat, silent.

David thought. "Is it what Rebecca said? About

Lucas? His time, it's up?"

"Yes and now he needs a *replacement*." She whispered the last word, revealing its true weight.

"But why me? Why not someone who wants this . . . contract?"

"Even da universe has its rules. Jared has disobeyed the order of his existence, as has da angel who corrupted him. Dhey must be challenged by someone of worth. Someone who knows right and senses evil. Ya'r grief, ya'r hardship has made ya . . . sensitive. The struggle tain't for nothin'. Dhey must be punished. Indeed."

"And what about me? What if I can't do this?"

Her face grew long and worrisome. "It's a light dwindling to an ember. Do not fail."

"I hope you're hungry, young David. Christine has created an array of delicious dishes and she doesn't take kindly to rejection. What? Did you see something out the window?"

David was no longer facing the chair where Mama had been sitting. He had moved quickly upon hearing Lucas' entry, but his eyes still fell on the place where she had vanished.

"An owl, I think," David replied. "I know there are quite a few up here."

"Bats, more likely. Nasty little buggers. They squeak and screech until you think you'll go mad. Drake says they live up in the eaves of the east wing." He placed two large oval dishes onto the table, removing their lids to reveal a pasta casserole and buttered asparagus spears. "I would have them exterminated, but those fish and game prats would fine me a sizeable bit."

"Fish and game? Do they even come up this way? Private property, isn't it?"

"It's the mountain, basically a preserve. I had to abide by a few wanker rules to build up here, but the privacy is worth it. Still, a ranger will pop by from time to time. Nosey yanks."

They both looked at the steaming food and the mere sight of it made David queasy. The parmesan cheese smelled rank to his senses. No way was he going to eat that.

"You should at least take a bite, mate," Jared whispered, leaning over the table. "She gets pretty pissy if she thinks its no good and that means none for me later, so do a bloke a favor, eh."

David nodded. *Sure, I'll do you a favor*, he thought. *I'll eat your girlfriend's dinner and then hurl it all over the table, blame it on the flu and have an excellent reason to haul ass out of here, muy pronto. Hell yeah, I'll do your favor all the way to PDX, dickhead.*

"Alright, gentlemen. Dig in."

Christine took her place next to Lucas and watched carefully for the initial response to a meal she had obviously taken great care in preparing. David shoveled the green stems onto his plate. He figured that if there was anything he could keep down it would be his veggies, but he didn't escape so easily.

"Why don't you just hand me your plate there, David and I will dish you up some of this fantastic cuisine?"

"I'm sure I can manage, Jared,"

"Not at all, the dish is scalding." Lucas grabbed David's plate from under him and began to scoop large sections of the red and white entree onto it. "Best to give you plenty now so as to not be shy for seconds." He beamed. He was enjoying this. They never should have sent this young, stupid boy to do their dirty work. He was a lamb to the slaughter, which didn't bother Lucas a bit. Lambs made the most fantastic screams.

"So naturally, I told Jared that I would make us dinner. That way you both would be equally equipped for the festivities." She smiled and held her glass to Jared who matched it with his own.

"It is a lovely meal, Christine," David began, shifting through his food so that it would appear to be eaten. Wasn't that what Melissa had done in the last few months when he had stopped noticing her? A meal here, an uneaten snack there? And what had she said the problem was really about, what struggle had she said food resembled? A struggle for control. "But I'm not feeling very well and I'm afraid I will have to excuse myself."

"Nonsense," Lucas scoffed, "we've gathered here especially for you. Christine's gone to all this trouble."

Christine pouted her beautiful lips to assure him that yes, she had, indeed, gone to a great deal of trouble and how rude he was for leaving. She could check those lips, David didn't care, he was getting the hell out of here.

"Yes, I realize and am very sorry, but I need to lie down."

Lucas stood up. "You can't just leave, mate."

David met his eyes. "Yes I can."

The protests followed David out of the room and by the time he reached the main corridor they had taken their effect. Was he sure? If he left tonight it would cost him his promotion, possibly his job. Was there really a threat? He was sure of the things he had seen, and not seen, for that matter. Mama was real, Rebecca was real. The dreams were, he thought, warnings, if anything and that was enough for him. He would hike down the mountain, take a taxi to PDX, get on a plane and never come back to the Pacific Northwest. He would lose his job and have to call the rental car company to pick up the Durango. They would insist that a representative visit him with a truckload of paperwork, which was fine. They could send the strawberry blonde.

He made his way back to his room and from beneath his bed he removed his slightly stuffed knapsack. After the trip with Brian, he always carried a loaded pack. Water, first aid kit, flashlight, matches and a knife had a permanent home in the North Face sack. David had decided to leave his laptop. He could send for it with the rest of his clothes *after* he was off the mountain and if he never got it back, well, it was old anyway. *No food?* his mind questioned. No, but the water should be enough. *Unless you can't make it down. Unless . . . something keeps you here.* Were those his thoughts? He spun around to face the rest of his room.

"I'll be fine," he said aloud.

Maybe, an inner voice responded.

"You can't keep me here!" He felt his voice crack in its struggle to be strong. "I'm going off this mountain tonight!"

Are you?

"Who are you?" he whispered, but there was nothing. He could almost sense that whatever, whoever had been with him, was now gone. David crouched beside the bed, holding his pack and for the last time dialed his phone.

"What the fuck did you do that for?" Lucas snapped.

"Oh, you'd rather cheat, what, like a mama's boy. Figures." Christine sipped her wine with an annoyed eagerness. Lucas knew that another bottle would soon follow, if not for her now, then definitely for him later. David's departure had surprised him and he, never one for surprises, already felt the unease of his miscalculation. Masterson should have eaten half his meal, at least his asparagus. Christine had covered every inch of his damn plate with powdered sleeping tablets, it would have only taken a bite. But he hadn't.

"I don't need to cheat, Christine," he breathed. "I have it under control." He rose from his seat and moved so that he was standing behind her. His hands rounded her shoulders and crept along her neck into her hair. She let her head fall back into his palms, smiling with slight enjoyment.

"He isn't like the other one, Jared."

"Perhaps. But I'm not worried."

"You should be."

He pulled her head back with a quick tug. A small

grunt of protest escaped her lips and her hands reached back, trying to loosen his grip.

"Listen to me, little star. You are here because I say you can be here. Do not make me change my mind."

"You wouldn't!" she cried.

"Yes, I would. They would forgive me, but you? No, there is only one place for traitors, Christine, only one place and it doesn't have any doors. Push me again and I will end you, sweetheart." He kissed her neck and released her hair. "Better get ready, darling. He will be leaving soon."

Her eyes shined with ethereal luminescence. "Yes, Jared."

CHAPTER THIRTEEN

"*M*artin?"

"David, what's wrong? Why are you calling me at home? Did you blow it? Godammit, Masterson! Why the fuck can't you ever do as you're told!"

"I'm in trouble, Martin, you gotta let me out of this story. He's ah, pretty crazy, boss I gotta tell ya. I'm fuckin' freakin' out."

"Okay, okay, just take it easy. What's the problem?"

What was the problem? Lucas hadn't actually done anything. David was staying in a beautiful room. He had been fed three fantastic meals on top of which high quality booze had followed and his host had been rather candid. What exactly was it?

"I think, I think he's on drugs."

"That's it? You're callin' me at home to tell me a rock star is on drugs? Are you fucking kidding me? You get your ass in gear, Dave. That story had better be on my desk in two days or I'm kicking you down to the goddamn mailroom!" He slammed down the receiver.

"Martin? Who was it?"

"Just one of my guys, honey. It's nothing."

His wife of 32 years had come into the room without him noticing. She wore a long cotton nightgown that was predominantly hidden by a heavy green robe. She was a robust woman with a chunky middle and arms to match. Her hair was bound at the top of her head in a loose bun and on her face a peach colored mask was drying.

"Don't be talking to them that way, Martin. It'll cause disrespect in the office."

"Yeah, I know, I know."

"What's the problem, anyway?"

"He wants out of a story."

"And you said 'no'? Why on earth not?" Her disapproval was obvious.

"Because, he needs to learn to stick it out."

"Stick it out? Like a roll of duck tape?" She shot him a contemptible look.

"Yeah, like a fucking roll of duck tape!"

"Don't take that tone with me Martin Mitchell. You've been crankier than a cat in a bath for two days."

She was right. He was pissy because he was tired. He hadn't been able to sleep. If that creature wasn't showing up in one place than it was showing up in another. Mirrors, windows, even in the shine of his new Mercedes and every time it was the same, talking without sound, those blue eyes looking at him and making him feel his soul cry in agony.

"Just tired."

"Well, I'm sure it has nothing to do with you staying up all night and sleeping damn near on top of me so neither one of us can get any rest and I bet that if there ever was a man who needed a toddler's nap in the whole world it would be you, Martin because my mama always said that a man without his rest is man fit to be tied and I believe it now because of the way you've been actin', I can't remember the last time you were so grumpy, except for the weekend that we spent with your sister up in Washington state, you know I believe that she really has it out for me the way that she kept on remarkin' about my dress, which I don't think she has any business doin' because her dress is as nasty as…"

She continued to talk as she walked out of the living room and into the kitchen, her slippers scuffing along the hardwood floors. He sighed and felt the last two days creep up over him. He was so tired, but every time he closed his eyes . . . there it was.

"Virginia? Do we still have that cough medicine that Dr. Parker gave us from Labor Day?"

Scuff, scuff.

"Are you getting sick? It's probably because you aren't sleeping and the body needs its rest, Martin as sure as the sun needs it."

"I want it to help me sleep."

"Oh. Yes, it's upstairs. You go get it and I'll pour you a nightcap." She looked over him once, slightly concerned and then headed back to the kitchen. He knew that she loved him, in her own way, as his own mother was fond of saying. But too many years had fallen between them and she had decided somewhere during that time to be mean, to be controlling and he, never wanting to leave her alone in the world, had conceded. Now he was a kept man, a pet who was allowed out for work and golf once a month with his brothers, but that was it. They attended her church, with her family, a band of equally chubby misfits who were as socially awkward as their waddling bodies. In all of California he found the one woman who was the farthest thing from the locales of which he was familiar. She was southern, traditional, stubborn, and he thought, a bit wrong. She had friends, women who were just like her: dominating, possessive and oblivious. Yet, she still loved him or loved the idea of him and when he asked her for the medicine she had picked up on his discomfort and had been kind. She wasn't cruel, just not the person she used to be. When they were younger she had been gentle, sweet and loving. She had been plump even then, but he hadn't cared because he loved her. Now he simply wanted that kindness back. He had seen a small reminiscent flicker of it in her response, but then it was gone.

As he climbed the stairs he passed the hallway mirror and without thinking looked into it. When had he become so old? His frame was trim, true, but his face showed his years, the lines running across his brow and around his mouth were deep and permanent. He was pale, minus the dark sacks below his eyes. Virginia had once given color to those cheeks. At one time she had come to bed every night naked and every night he would touch her warm body and feel the happiness that makes life full. He would make love to her and enjoy her. They weren't newlyweds at that time, nor even as comfortable in themselves as they were now, but it had been great. He had been happy. And like all men, wanted that feeling, all of that feeling, to bless his life once more.

It wasn't until he left the mirror and reached the top of the stairs that he realized the change. He inched slowly back to the wall fixture and peered into its glossy surface. Only his reflection shone. The creature was gone.

David didn't have a whole lot of time. It was already getting late and he was sure it would take him a fair amount of hours to get off Lucas' property. How many acres was it? One hundred and fifty-four? Fifty-five? If he was lucky he would find the shortest length between those acres and Government Camp. It was always ski season up here on Hood and David knew the hotels would be up and running no matter what time he came out of the woods. He gave a brief snort. Coming out of the woods. Like Dorothy and her fucking little rat dog. He changed his shoes. His hiking boots were a bit worn, but fantastically broken in and David felt an ounce of comfort just by putting them on. He had been wearing these boots the last time he was in trouble and they had carried him to safety, dry feet and all. He hoped their success would be repeated. If not, then nothing would give him more pleasure then to be buried in the damn things. He snorted again. At least Brian would be able to ID him without difficulty, "Yup, officer, that's him alright. He always did like those damn boots."

He stood in front of the bed and took inventory. He felt as if he was missing something. His right hand moved to the back pocket of his jeans. His eyes squeezed shut with the confirmation of an absence.

Wallet. Where had he left his damn wallet? At home its place was on his dresser next to his watch and phone, but where had he put it when he got here?

Durango.

"Who said that?" His voice was soft and almost inaudible. "Please, who are you?"

Durango.

"How do you know that? Please, help me get out of here."

He waited for a moment, hoping something would follow. He held his breath, concentrating on the silence and when the voice spoke again David understood it perfectly.

Go now.

David grabbed the pack and quickly slipped out of the room.

*

"Martin! What in god's name do you think you are doing? Come to bed already. You're always lollygagging around."

Martin Mitchell was standing in his bathroom with his back to the mirror and his head buried in his cupped hands. He lowered his hands and looked at Virginia. She was sitting upright in bed, her gigantic bosom creating a large mound under the blankets she held firmly to her neck.

"Nothing, tulip. Go to sleep, I'll be there in a minute." He was relieved when, for the first time in a long time she abided by his instructions and lay back down. A couple of minutes later he heard her breathing slow to a rhythmic flow that always meant sleep. He closed the door.

He didn't like that the monster was gone. It had been there for a reason. He knew there must be something, something important, something urgent. Virginia had made the nightcap and he had poured it into the fichus plant in the den. He wanted it, the almost creamed liquor that bit into his senses just as it was running down his throat and deep into his stomach. He wanted the carelessness and freedom that came with the numbness of a double tall on the rocks, but he couldn't tonight. He had work to do and he wanted to be clear. He thought he could bring it back. He thought that if he focused he could summon it and if he was able to endure the sight of it, might be able to understand what it was saying.

Martin's heart was steady. He had never served in the military, but as a third generation firefighter he had learned to concentrate and dull his susceptibility to his surroundings. Get in, get out is what his dad had told him on his first day. He had done that. For eight years he went in and came right back out again, usually a body or two heavier, but when his dad, granddad and brother were killed in a hospital fire, Martin quit the job, went back to school and became an editor. He wasn't a hero anymore, not even to his own wife. Now, he was only a man behind a desk, a man who spent his days and nights reading what others wrote. His time had passed, but if he could just do this one thing, he knew that the heart that beat so strongly before still remained in his chest. All he had to do was turn around . . .

The hallway from David's room was clear and quiet. Were they still in the dining room? He couldn't hear anything. His heartbeat thudded against his chest in an almost deafening pound. What was the fastest way to the front door? He thought that down the backstairs into the kitchen and through the den to the foyer was the way to go. He would probably be able to hear them if they were in the den, kitchen or dining room while he was still on the staircase. He could wait there, wait for an opportunity.

He raced down the hall to the slightly hidden narrow staircase that led to the kitchen. He couldn't help but wonder why a man who let the help (Drake) walk around in full view would want a servant's staircase to the kitchen. Stairs like these were meant to conceal undesirables, servants, slaves or anyone not fit for the main staircase. A sneaky way to slip in and out without being noticed. The history of them was grim, but David felt great appreciation for the subtle nature of the steps. They would hide him and if need be, would allow him to creep back to his room undetected.

The slope of the steps was steep and David's nervous legs trembled with each descent. Three quarters of the staircase was dark from the hall, but the last ten steps were illuminated by the kitchen light. He was two steps above the pale floorboards when Christine stopped him.

He didn't even see the hair this time, just the eyes. Pleading, horrid and feverish, they were more blue than the oceans and deeper than the sky and Martin felt as if he would be lost inside them. Cruel, yet enchanting they were. His mind screamed tearful sobs, but his heart refused to budge. He dropped his eyes to the creature's mouth, which moved dramatically. He couldn't see any lips, just magnificent white teeth that beamed in contrast to its red tongue. It kept repeating the same thing over and over. Martin's head began to ache. He vaguely noticed his hands clenching the edge of the counter, the skin over each knuckle split open in red ravines. Trouble? Was that it? Was that one of the words?

"*Can't, understand,*" he groaned, but the creature continued with his ritual, its mouth widening and closing in escalated impatience. The pain was growing. His vision was blurring, then the tight tunnel of concentration broke. Martin collapsed to the floor, his head connecting with the rim of the toilet bowl.

He was in his bed. He reached up to feel the knot where the porcelain had clipped his skull. There was a lump, but it didn't hurt.

"Martin? Are you okay?"

"Yes, Virg," he stopped. Virginia was standing over him, a cool compress in hand, but . . . she looked different. "Virginia?"

"Yes. What is it sweetheart? Does your head hurt? I can get you another aspirin. You do have quite a lump there, Mitch."

Mitch? She hadn't called him that since college. He loved that name. Martin was his perverted uncle on his mother's side. Martin was your math teacher. Martin was your dentist, but Mitch, oh hell no, Mitch was a fireman. Mitch was a baseball player or a construction worker who slept with younger women and drank whiskey for breakfast.

"I fell."

"Yeah, I know. You were doing pull-ups in the doorframe again, weren't you?"

"Pull-ups?"

"Don't lie, Mitch. A woman notices when a man has been working out." He was dumbfounded. Who in the world was this crazy broad? "But, I guess I shouldn't complain. You've never looked better, honey."

She put the cold compress across his forehead, sat down on the bed and began to stroke his leg.

"Virginia, I don't know what-"

"Don't worry about a thing, Mitch. I called the house and your brother is going to fill in for you tonight."

"My brother? Virginia, I think you have completely lost it."

"No, no, none of that now. You just relax and let me take care of you."

He rested his head against his pillow, his eyes still tracking her delicate movements. Even as he watched her he felt suspended, sleepy and when her mouth made contact with his stomach Martin let his eyes close for good.

CHAPTER FOURTEEN

"What are you doing, Mr. Masterson?" Christine's voice was soft and flirty, not loud, but substantial in the silence in which David was standing. "You might as well come out, I know you're there." He paused, hoping she would second-guess her conviction. "Jared has gone to bed. Come out and have a glass of wine with me." He set down his pack and continued into the light. She smiled with great amusement. Women always enjoyed being right and this one was no different. David watched as that smile grew into a sweeping grin. "Let me guess, you're hungry. Well, I would imagine. You didn't eat a thing at dinner."

"Yes, I'm sorry about that."

"Never mind. You can join me for some vino roso and cheese."

David placed a hand over his stomach, "I'm not feeling up to it actually, still a bit shaky. I don't want to bother you. I was just coming down for some water-"

"In your hiking boots?" The smile had faded, but the grin still lingered, mean and knowing.

"I was going to get some fresh air, clear the sinuses, you know."

"Best of luck, Jared set the alarm. Does every night. Set it off a few times myself. Believe me, there won't be a person from here to Bend that won't know you were going AWOL."

"Surely you can let me out?"

"Sure I could, if I wanted you to get out." She was shrinking the distance between them as she spoke and suddenly she was right in front of him, breathing him in, stalking him.

"You have a problem with letting a guy go for a

walk?"

"Yeah, I do. Walking alone on Hood at night isn't a very smart thing to do. Animals and all that."

"I can handle it."

She laughed, "Yeah, that's what they all say. I could go with you. . ." She was so close to him. He could smell her hair, almost taste her perfume.

"That's sweet," he said, taking a step back. "But a smart man also does not take his boss's girl out for a moonlight stroll. Guess I'll just call it a night."

She looked at him, concentrating and then beamed again, "Good night, then."

He headed up the staircase and was just beyond the light when she spoke again, "And David, don't forget your pack."

The soft pads of Christine's feet made gentle little whispers on the tile in the foyer. She ascended the stairs with light, playful hops. She knew he would run. She knew he was too weak to tough it out and now she couldn't wait to tell Jared that the chase had begun. He had taken David's exit from dinner as a sure sign of nervousness and was convinced that the young writer would return to his room where he would stay, scared, until Jared was ready to finish him. Christine had disagreed and decided to remain in the kitchen waiting for David while Jared retired to his bedroom. Jared was smart, but Christine simply knew more. She had chosen him because of his arrogance, intellect and selfishness, but she was beginning to tire of him. He was an impatient little boy, completely unaware of the sins and crimes in which he had partaken while in her company. He was just a man, not an angel. He did not know the truths and rules of the universe as she did and it was only a matter of time before they destroyed him. But there was no need to wait and have him further jeopardize her place here. She would do this with him and when they were done, she would kill him.

She danced from step to step, the contents of her wine glass swishing gently against the crystal cup. She raised her eyes to the second floor landing and saw Emily standing there, Barbie doll still in hand.

"You're supposed to be in bed, sweetheart."

"No more," Emily replied.

Christine's face tightened.

"Go to bed, Emily."

"No more," she repeated. She held the doll out in front of her, its lifeless legs dangling below Emily's grip. An expression of realization crossed Christine's face.

"I didn't know," she whimpered. "Please, I didn't know!"

"No more." Emily turned to the handrail and without emotion or word dropped the doll over the side, down to the empty foyer. Christine's eyes, wide in horror and wet with tears, followed the doll's descent. Emily watched as the doll made contact with the floor and promptly disappeared. She looked to Christine with unaffected eyes. She saw the regret, the entitlement and the rage that lay beneath those tears. As the last watery drop hit her perfect cheek, Christine vanished.

Emily sighed. Another one lost. Hopefully she would be the last, but that would all depend on the man.

David's room was exactly as he had left it, but he felt as if someone had been there.

"Rebecca?"

Nothing.

"Mama?"

Nothing. No one was there. He concentrated harder.

"Help. I know you can hear me. Please help me."

Again, silence. He looked around the room. What was it? It was as if he could see the fingerprints, feel the body heat of the person who had been there. But what had changed? He turned in circles. Bed.

Fireplace. Chair. Dresser. Window. Bed. Back again. Window! He leapt across the room to the wooded pane. The large frames were slightly parted. He tugged at one and it swung open. The cold night air raced into the room. It was damp with rain and thick with promise. No alarm, nothing but his heartbeat. He looked down. At least a twenty-foot drop, he thought. There was a lip separating the two storeys, but it was ten feet below his window's edge. He would have to lower himself onto it and pray that the native combination of rain and mold had not made it slick.

He tightened his pack to his back and swung his leg over the window pane. He would be going down feet first, with his chest hugging the side of the house. He thought this to be the simplest approach, although with his back to the driveway someone could see him and he wouldn't know. The side of the house was wet and his grip a bit weak, but he let his feet slide below him until finally they connected with the thin stone ledge. He spread his arms out to each side, his fingers searching for cracks to cling to. He brought his right knee down onto the ledge, letting his left follow suit. His hands lowered to the lip's edge and very slowly he began to drop his legs over the side. A minute later he was standing below his bedroom window. Not bad, he thought. No broken bones and barely a sound. He took a last look at his window, one of several in the house bright with light.

"Thank you," he said.

He crept down the brick driveway to where the Durango was parked. It seemed like years since he had seen it. He fumbled through his pack searching for the OMSI key ring. The search was torturous, but quickly concluded. He hadn't forgotten it. He pulled out the circular metal pendant that read OREGON MUSEUM OF SCIENCE AND INDUSTRY in small white letters. Below the inscription was a picture of a submarine. A small part of him ached momentarily.

This place had a whole new meaning for him now. It was no longer the home of summer hikes and fireworks over the bridges. Now Oregon meant fear, evil, a place where people like Lucas could taint him. Jared Lucas had ruined this special place for him.

He shoved the singular key into the Durango's passenger door and turned it. The interior light went on as bright as the sun in the dark evening. David quickly jumped onto the seat and closed the door. He hunched below the glove compartment.

"Damn light, damn, stupid light!" He breathed, hoping that the light or the sound of the door closing hadn't attracted any attention. He popped his head up, his eyes still adjusting from the momentary shine from the truck's ceiling. He scanned the driveway, the front door, the windows, all was sound. When he felt it was safe, he sat upright and opened the compartment.

He should have known. After all, any man who is holding another man as a prisoner would take that prisoner's ID. It was probably the first thing he did. David eyes fell on the console. The ignition plate had been removed as had the pedals and David guessed, most likely a few engine parts. Every doubt that he had, every drilling question about his perception of this situation burst into flames in his mind like a burning sacrifice. Rebecca was right, Mama Legna was right. They had been telling the truth. Lucas intended for him to stay here, stay until . . . what? What was going to happen?

"So there's no way . . ." His heart slowed for a moment and he thought he might faint. "Oh god, get me outta here."

Then, movement. He couldn't see exactly what it was, but his vision caught it all the same. Someone was in his room, their elongated shadow beaming through the window. He inched down the seat as low as his 6-foot frame would allow. The figure was moving rapidly, its outline bouncing from wall to wall.

"He's looking for you." A voice boomed from the backseat. David whipped around to see Drake, legs extended across the seat, his back and head resting comfortably against the window.

"What the fuck are you doing? Get me the hell outta here, man!"

"Quiet!" Drake snapped. "You wanna bring him out here? Not that he isn't going to find his way sooner or later."

David was quiet, a strained grimace of fear and sweat worked deep lines along his brow. Drake had forgotten how young he was. The lines had barely begun their work. His eyes were bright and new, not the eyes of a man who has seen sixty years of life. He was just a boy and those eyes weren't capable of enduring . . . but he somehow felt they would withstand.

"You need to focus, David. Jared's control over you, over this situation, is based on you not losing your head."

"It's not my head I'm worried about." Their eyes met. "How can he take my soul, Drake? I mean, just take it? Isn't it mine?"

"Yes and no. Your soul is part of the universe and just like any living being it can be imprisoned."

"So, I'll know? If he gets his way and takes my soul and uses it to live, I'll know? Trapped inside his mind? What? Like a fucking ghost? There, but not there? How can God let this happen?"

"God is the center of the universe. This is just one thing of billions occurring in that universe and I hate to break it to you, but it is not the worst."

David tried to absorb the enormity of Drake's revelation. "Does God even care? Why is he letting Jared do this?"

"There are so many things and so many needs, most of them we create in our efforts to dominate one another. She does what she can when she can, but if she *did* all the time we would never learn and some of us still don't. Jared is well aware that God will not be stepping in to save you. He is counting on it."

"So how the hell does that help me?"

"You can do this on your own. There is a strength at the center of every human being. It is the will to survive, the need to continue, the passion for life. That alone will get you through tonight. By morning, it will be over, one way or the other."

Drake had kind eyes, but his words held David and he couldn't bring himself to look away. "What do I do?"

Drake lowered his feet to the floorboards and scooted closer to David, his glance occasionally darting past him to the house. "He is going to try to drive you to unconsciousness. You must stay awake and find your way down the mountain."

David's mind clicked. "That's what Rebecca said, she told me that I was, was vulnerable in my sleep."

"Yes, they attack the body when it's asleep because it is the only time the mind will be susceptible to those types of horrors."

"How will he do it? I mean, I'm safe as long as I'm awake, right?"

"It's not that easy. He will try to tempt you and you must fight through it. You must not resign yourself or your mind." Drake shifted his weight until his face was within inches of David's. "Don't go into your mind. No daydreaming, no lost in thought. Focus, but don't concentrate. Those are states of neutrality. It is just as if you were sleeping."

"How can I not think for *Christ's* sake? Focus but not concentrate? What the fuck does that mean?"

"It means own your mind, dammit! Don't let him in! Don't let anybody in. The true state of living is being aware of the present. When people stare off into space, when they create and entertain dialogue in their heads they are succumbing, they are escaping! But what they don't realize is that alone leaves them open to all the horrors that make up the uncertainty that man has labeled evil. Paranoia, hatred, anger, vengeance are the products of unfocused minds. It is only when we see our surroundings for what they really are, that we are able to deal with them in a way that is sincere to humanity. A way that is truly human."

"So no thought, fine. What about the morning? What if I find help before then?"

"You won't. Honestly son, it's not in your favor. But if you run you might have a chance."

"How long do I have, I mean, how long even if I don't reach the highway by morning?"

"That depends on you. There is eight hours of darkness left. Jared will fight until the very last star has vanished."

"Is it enough just to survive? Can't I just hole up with you somewhere on the mountain, wait for sunrise?"

"No, I am not allowed to help you escape, which is what you must do. Get off this mountain, find the main road. It is the only way out."

"But what about you? Emily? And that Christine woman?"

"I will take care of Emily and Emily will take care of Christine." He shot a look at the house again. "It won't be long now. You better get going."

David started to adjust his backpack straps. "Don't bother with that. You should leave it here."

"What? Are you crazy? I'm gonna need water and-"

"If you are alive come morning, then you will be in a beautiful hotel room surrounded by bottled water. If Jared wins you'll be dead and it won't matter anyway. Either way, the pack will only weigh you down. Leave it."

David shed the canvass bag along with its comfort. He felt as if he were deliberately making the same mistake that had almost gotten him killed a couple years before. Drake gestured to him to put it down and David did. At least he had his boots.

"Head down the driveway. When you reach the gate, go down the embankment to the right of it. When you reach the gully, head south. From there on, you are on your own."

"Drake?"

"Yes?"

"Has this ever happened before?"

"Yes, son, it has."

"Did he make it?"

"No."

"I will." The words were out and even though he did not feel any confidence behind them, David was comforted by their hope.

"Good luck, son."

Drake slipped out of the car on one side and David on the other. Drake disappeared into the rose garden without a sound. David knew that Drake had endangered himself and maybe others to counsel him. He was special, not quite as strong in presence as Rebecca, but there was something. As David quickly crept down the driveway he realized that as they had opened the doors of the Durango the light in the truck's cab had not gone on.

(HAPTER FIFTEEN

Because his visitor had left his laptop and clothes, Lucas knew immediately that David wasn't planning on driving down the mountain. There hadn't been anything that he didn't anticipate, but Christine had been correct in her assessment of David's discomfort and she had known long before him that David would be leaving tonight, on foot. A hell of a lot of good it did her, he thought to himself, rummaging through the bedroom, occasionally kicking a piece of furniture in frustration. She was gone. He had felt her leave. The cold hold over him that was neither female nor human had ceased. He didn't know if she had fled or was taken, either way he was left to work alone. Mr. Masterson had left quickly, that was obvious, but it wasn't until a draft from the open window blew against his face that Lucas realized how. He tore to the window, covering the room in giant strides. His head emerged into the night air, his eyes first looking out then down.

"Son of a bitch."

The scuff marks from David's shoes shone like rough abrasions on the house's stonework. Jared felt heat rising to his temples. He dropped his head below his squared shoulders and closed his eyes. At first, only the wind spoke, but moments later a word fell on his ears clear and crisp. *Emily.*

"Oh Mitch, I love you so much."

It had been a long time since Virginia voiced her affection for her husband; to Martin it felt like decades. He did love her and all he ever wanted was her love in return.

"Vee, my sweet, sweet wife, you're so beautiful." They lay together, bodies wet with sweat, hands interlaced, eyes locked on each other.

"Let's never be the way we've been, Mitch. Not ever again."

"Oh, I've missed you so much," his eyes swam dreamily over her soft, delicate complexion. She seemed more stunning than ever and he felt a hopeful rejoicing in his chest. So many years had been wasted and now, after all that time, he had his wife back. "There's so many things I want to say because I don't want this to end," he could feel his face twitch with emotion. "I was wrong so many times, Vee-"

"Shhh, that doesn't matter now. We are here, together, and I love you." Her eyes were so captivating to him, her face so gentle. He was so enamored by her that he almost didn't see the figure enter the room. It came from the hall, out of the darkness and into the candlelight. Martin sat up, throwing his arms over Virginia in protection.

"Get out of here!" he hollered, but the monster continued to walk towards the bed. "Don't worry, Virginia, I'm here. . . I won't let him hurt you!" His voice was shaky and to his surprise, was the only one.

"You can't do anything," he heard Virginia hiss from behind him. He turned and saw that her once beautiful face was pulled taut in a snarl.

"Stand," the creature said.

Martin panicked. He looked at Virginia then to the monster and then back to Virginia again. "What?"

"Stand," it repeated.

Martin slowly pulled back the sheets and slid off the bed. He had been naked, but now he was wearing his pajamas. He touched the side of his head and felt moisture. It had been a lie.

"No time for dreaming," the monster said, "find the light, save the heart that beats for all of us, and at last you will know peace." It turned and walked into the bathroom. Martin looked at the bed. The real Virginia lay sleeping on her side, cotton nightgown, curlers intact, snoring. He followed the creature and stopped just shy of the bathroom's threshold.

"How?" he asked.

The creature looked at him, blue eyes deep and sorrowful as if holding the screams and cries of every abandoned newborn. Martin's mind throbbed at the sight of them, his soul shuddering.

"The trees."

"I don't understand-" He crossed the threshold and just as his feet made contact with the Spanish tile the creature disappeared and Martin found himself lying on the floor next to the toilet. He opened his eyes widely, trying to bring them into focus. He managed to get upright and hoisted himself onto the toilet seat. His head hurt from where he had cracked it on the porcelain and small drops of red had found their way down his neck, staining the collar of his pajamas. None of it had been real. Virginia, their passion, her caring, it was all a dream. It had felt real, but it wasn't. Martin looked down at his wedding ring and felt a cold vine of grief wrap itself around his heart. A tear escaped his left eyelid and with furious hurt he quickly wiped it away. He stood, went to the sink, dampened a towel and began to clean his wound. It hurt and Martin would have to see Dr. Parker in the morning for a couple of stitches, but he thought it would be fine until morning. He threw the towel on the floor, switched off the light and shuffled to bed.

The hallway was dark, but Lucas could see perfectly. The heat from inside his body seemed to escape through his eyes, illuminating the dark with its potent projection. Emily's room was in the east wing of the house, quite a distance from his own. When she first came to live with him he instinctively prepared a room close to his, but reconsidered her placement after Christine's first night in the house. He valued his privacy and she appeared to prefer isolation, so without protest he moved her to the far end of the house. Her new living quarters were made up of several rooms; a parlor with a fireplace, a playroom constructed into a miniature castle, a bedroom and a private bath. Drake had bought and restored an old rod iron, red school desk and had placed it in the parlor for her daily tutoring sessions. Lucas had assumed, mostly because he didn't think she was capable of telling him, that she liked her rooms. She very rarely left them and often times it was only to sit in the rose garden that was considered hers anyway.

Tonight he found her just as he had expected, curled up into a small lump under a pink comforter, her fingers folded tightly over a tiny doll with brown hair. He rounded the bed and sat down beside her knees. She, like all children, looked angelic in her sleep, the weight of the world absent and unknown to her quiet dreams.

Why had the voice said *Emily* to him? She had not helped Masterson out of the house. She had no doubt been there sleeping since dinner, he was certain. Even if she had taken to David, which Lucas thought was highly unlikely, she wouldn't have had the mind to suspend the alarm and let him out.

Despite her disability, Emily had shown an interest in anything with buttons. DVD players, microwaves, light fixtures and the control panel to the house's alarm system all caught her eye and held her attention until she was competent in their function. Lucas had reset the alarm five times before resigning to her. After all, she hardly ever left the house and had never ventured beyond the garden. He didn't think there was any danger in her turning the alarm on and off as she pleased and had in fact assigned her to arming the house every night before bed. It was part of her routine and Lucas had faith in its repetition.

Perhaps he hadn't heard anything. It might have been his mind's way of reminding him to check on her. Either way, Emily was here, sleeping, uncomplicated and quiet and he would pursue Masterson on his own while she slept.

Lucas crept out of the floral room, closing the door behind him. By the time he had returned to his room for his shoes, Emily was out of bed, dressed and negotiating the latch on the attic door in her closet. The young man would need help and even if she couldn't give it to him, she would need to be somewhere where she could see the occurring events.

The attic door was in the ceiling of her coat closet, its small square outline made practically invisible by strategically placed wallpaper. There was a stairway entrance into the attic from a door in the hallway. But the door was directly adjacent to her uncle's room and when an exploration of the attic had lead her to this alternate entrance, Emily ceased using the hallway door altogether. An antique bureau with a marble countertop, normally the home of her mother's porcelain dolls, was her stepping ladder. Emily had gotten into the habit of removing the dolls and then putting them back, should her uncle ever become curious about a used bureau in her closet. But then it became clear that not only would he never notice such a thing (as it had no direct effect upon him whether she used a family bureau or not), but that he would only upon occasion visit her room, let alone her coat closet.

When she stood on the bureau, her midsection rose into the ceiling and through the square opening. She pulled herself up backward, allowing the bottom of her jeans to land on the floor of the attic. She scooted backwards until her knees, calves and finally her feet were clear of the opening. She closed the hatch door and locked it. She didn't think her uncle knew about her special door, but there was no reason to chance it.

The attic was big, but filled. Furniture covered in plastic, spare instruments transferred from the studio, a trunk with her father's old records, B.O.C., Iron Butterfly and the like, a china hutch, a stripped pool table, a chest from Denmark, all making unfriendly lumps of shadows on the dusty floorboards. She was always amused by humans' material possessions. It was, after all, only plastic and wood.

The attic's main window was rather small, but opened out onto a stoop just big enough for Emily to perch. She zipped up her jacket and wrapped her arms around her knees, placing her doll in the small space between her sneakers. The evening was brisk. She thought the coming hours would bring a heavy fog, which was good for him. She knew he would need its protection. She closed her eyes. In her ears his heartbeat sounded. It was faint at first, but then the rhythm became steadier and finally solid in presence. She opened her eyes and looked out. Somewhere in the dark the light was running and with it, the only chance for peace.

*

David hit the gate with surprising speed. It only seemed a few minutes since he left Drake, but in pure adrenaline his feet had carried him quickly to the wall of iron and stone and now his eyes were running along the words that had triggered the beginning of this nightmare. Lament Hill. He couldn't help but stare. To lament, to confess, to feel suffering. So many things in his life were encompassed by that one word. It seemed to mock him, to coax him into questioning himself. An owl screeched from one of the stone pillars and David jumped in nervous anxiety. It gave him a placid stare from its cocked head and then took flight. David watched its shape disappear into nothingness.

"Move it or lose, asshole," he muttered, taking to the right side of the drive until the toes of his boots tipped the edge of a prominent, dark gully. He turned and gave the words one last look. They were already trying for him, already working to distract him, dummying him into subconscious, taking his mind for their own. "Fuck you," he said, raising the middle finger on his smooth left hand. The night was still and the gate didn't reply. David began to descend down the slope. He slid and slipped a few times, but within seconds was at the bottom of the gully.

CHAPTER SIXTEEN

The ground at the bottom of the gully was damp. Moss was prevalent, covering rocks and tree trunks, reflecting the few moonbeams that shot through the canopy in electric rays. David wished he had brought a flashlight. The pack hadn't been that heavy and he didn't know why he had allowed Drake to persuade him to leave it behind. He was only able to see about ten yards ahead of him, which didn't keep his feet from occasionally tripping over a protruding rock or fallen tree branch. He would never make it unless he picked up some speed. He looked above him and saw that the opposite side of the gully had a clear edge, less growth. He figured that if he stuck to the edge of the drop he could follow the gully bottom without the obstacle of forest debris.

He climbed up the embankment, going at an angle so as to continue his progression forward. When he reached the top he was gratified to see that the edge of the embankment was free of debris and noticeably more level than the gully floor. David felt a small bite of pride at his accomplishment and began a steady jog along the embankment's edge. If he kept a fair pace he could be down the mountain or at least to the highway in a few hours.

David was not, by nature, a runner. He was fond of walking and often went for strolls around his neighborhood in the late evening. When Melissa left, he had felt the need to exorcise his pain and running proved to be a quick, easy way. His feet pounding the pavement, every step pressing his anger and frustration out of his body and into the cement. It felt like blooding the fifth grade bully, like making that first contact hit in football, like jumping into a pool, like the embrace of being inside a woman, all these things that brought out the anguish that riddled a man's insides.

Only now, there was no release. He felt no relief, only a slight disdain for the force that had placed him in these woods, was making him run, ruining the pleasure he had derived from this place that had once been a second home to him. The trees were not beautiful, but rather dominating as they hung overhead, standing still despite his pace. They did not whip by like the ones along his favorite path near the Willamette, nor sparse like those planted by the city of Portland to pay homage to the local nature. These trees were brooding, intimidating, watching. His legs pumped and his mind registered a small flare of expulsion. The anger he was feeling slowly began to escape. He moved faster, his stride elongated, his brow secreting. He was nobody. He had no one. He wasn't going to make it out of this forest. God was not going to help him. He was alone. He could see the path ahead, but his mind watched as flashes of disappointment reeled in his brain. Images that had lay dormant, now coming out in bursts David could not control. First there was his father, standing in his garage, wiping the grease off a well worn hammer handle.

"It can't be helped son. They said they could try, but it has already spread. My dad had it and his dad had it, guess it only makes sense for me to. Hell, I got nine years more than either of 'em. Looks like when it is all said and done it'll be ten."

"What can I do, Pop?"

"Nothing, just be strong and take care of your mother for me. No more of this, Dave. You go help her. I'm gonna stay out here awhile."

David's heart began to hurt as it hammered rapidly in his chest. Then there was Brian, rain soaked and coughing, lost in the woods.

"It's getting hard to breathe, boss." His arms were wrapped around his knees, his back pressed against a rock. "Maybe you should make a go for it without me, could be faster."

"I don't think so, asshole, if I return without ya Grace would have my nuts in a vice." They had laughed, which triggered a coughing fit and David saw for a second time how his friend had looked those two years ago. His back arched, face crimson with pressure, as he dispelled a wad of mucus that hit the ground and finally soothed his lungs.

"On second thought, stay here, don't want to die alone. So tired." David thought it was a miracle that he hadn't died. Brian's fever began to climb three hours later and his body had shook with rampant chills. With each convulsion David had felt death creeping over his friend, but they had made it. Perhaps that was the one time God was able to help him. He had used up his pass. From then on he had been on his own. No help. It explained a lot.

David stopped. How long had he been running? He looked to his left. No embankment. No gully. He squinted in the dark, but his heartbeat sent dots across his vision, which was smeared by sweat that poured from his forehead. He spun in a circle, but saw nothing. He had been inside his head. They had tricked him into remembering and now, he was lost.

Jared Lucas had loved his house. He had gone to great lengths to make it the house he thought someone of his position deserved; a beautiful, isolated compound controlled solely by him. But as he exited its enormous front doors, he felt a discontent with its ineptitude. How was Masterson able to escape? The slick side of the house should have guaranteed a harsh drop to the gravel driveway, but instead it would seem that David had descended and fled without any level of difficulty. The next house, Lucas thought to himself, the next house will be better.

He knew that Masterson would head downhill to the gate and his senses told him that Drake was nearby, perhaps in the garden. It was interesting the way his mind worked, the images that came to it telling him where people were and sometimes, where they were going. Christine had called it a gift, a small token of his new enlightened state, but it was inconsistent. If Emily had changed the code on the house alarm and refused to tell her uncle what it was, Lucas was not able to mentally see her the next time she approach the key pad. If she was aware of his interest, he had no insight and his gift was useless. He was sure that Drake had alerted Masterson to the dangers of leaving his mind open, but Lucas could still sense David's rapid thoughts, running in circles somewhere in the gully below the drive. He was panicking and Lucas knew that fear was soon to follow.

He jogged down the drive, steady in pace and focus, looking for any sign of movement in the surrounding trees. When he reached the gate he turned left and began trudging down the slope of the ravine that dropped fifty feet to the mossy forest floor. There were no broken branches, no boot prints that Lucas could see, no evidence at all of Masterson's passing. Lucas hunkered down on his heels, rested a hand to the cool ground and closed his eyes. He concentrated. He could see trees, the night's darkness, and subtle streams of moonlight parting between them, but they were all stationery. Masterson was not moving.

David knew the feeling immediately as it grew inside him. Being lost was like drowning, every moment worse then the one before. Dying by inches, struggle, disorientation, and the unmistakable feeling of being completely screwed. He had been lost before and just like now it had been in the vast forests of Oregon. The swallowing depth of unclaimed trees whose trunks never saw daylight. The unforgiving black that was never penetrated by starlight. A world devastating and merciless. David felt weakened by its enormity and his inability to navigate in its diabolical distinction. Every tree looked the same, every rock molded to a fallen log without any notable characteristic. He must have run too far to the right-

"I didn't cross back over the gully,' he said aloud. "It should be close, somewhere to the left." He walked as the deduction circulated in his mind and the clarity of his thinking brought comfort. As he walked he understood Drake's point. As long as he controlled his thoughts, not the other way around, he would feel strong and be strong. His walk felt purposeful and his mind aware. It wasn't fifteen minutes before David reached the gully's edge. "Damn straight,' he smirked, creeping once more down the embankment. Just as before the floor of the gully was riddled with fallen logs and unearthed rocks. David sighed with annoyance and began to push his way through the debris.

The next hour was very slow. The path at the center of the two slopes had not seen enough rain water to wash away the forest's remnants and David began to feel discouraged by his slow process. Wherever Lucas was and whenever he had left the house, he was bound to catch up with David at this pace. David stopped and sat on the damp ground. His eyes had completely adjusted to the dark but he was still struggling to identify shapes from shadows. His hands hurt, slightly bloodied from his labor and his undershirt was soaked with perspiration. He lifted his hands close to his face and looked at his scratched knuckles. A couple of old scars had been opened up. His eyes glanced over each wound, the last of which was a jagged abrasion running from knuckle to knuckle on his left ring finger. A wedding band would have taken the brunt of it. But there was no band on his finger. No golden symbol of commitment, no life shared with another. Melissa had wanted to get married, he had wanted to marry her. But Dad's death had finally come, he thought. After all that time and all that hope, Dad had passed away quietly in his own bed, the cancer, ironically, dormant and small. Melissa had been patient. She had put up with his grief. Tears at first, then endless rage and hatred for the world, which he didn't think would ever completely leave him, but after a few months the anger gave way to a silence, a lack of concern or care. He didn't give a shit about anything. He ate and more often drank and lived on the couch, week after week, until months had flown by and he hadn't even stepped out of his front door to get the paper. She had waited, had endured with him, but then the patience had run out. She would ask him to go for a walk with her, to eat dinner at the kitchen table, hell to at least please sleep in the same bed as her and he had refused. Not a loud protest, just 'no'. Brian had tried too and they had tried together, out of love for him, but it wasn't enough. When their conjoined efforts led to mutual affection David didn't even notice. It wasn't until a week after she left that David had found a note on his dresser, its words snapping him out of his grief and injecting him with hers.

  She said she missed him. She said he was her joy and hope and that his life had enriched hers had made her feel completely happy. She said that everybody loses someone, that he was tragic, but not lost. She had wanted to know why he had given up on her, that his rejection was cruel and endless. She said that she felt like dying, that his misery was shared and amplified in her heart by his inability to communicate his thoughts to her. She said he was the greatest disappointment she had ever known and perhaps some day she would forgive him for his devastating selfishness. She had said all these things and he had cried after reading them. Now, sitting in the dark alone, he felt himself move from the present to that day in their bedroom. He had stood there in front of his redwood dresser, wearing a bathrobe and stale pajamas, crying, aching so badly from the inside out that his hands shook. Even now he could feel the weight of the paper between those unsteady fingers. The weight of the robe crushing down on his shoulders.

"David."

He turned and saw Melissa standing in the door. His heart seized, his eyes wide.

"But, you *didn't* come back," he stammered. "I read the letter, called you at Brian's, but you *didn't* come back."

"We can change that, David. It doesn't have to end with me leaving. We can be together." She walked toward him, her perfume reached his senses, just before her hands wrapped her delicate fingers around his neck. "I know you loved me. I just couldn't wait any longer."

"I, can't, this didn't happen," his lips moved, but the words came out in fits and starts.

"That doesn't matter. David, kiss me."

She kissed his lips, her soft chin grazing his four day stubble. Her body was warm and sweet. He drew his fingers in and out of her hair, its fine light weight tickled his palms and he felt a surge of intensity overcome his body.

David.

He pulled away from her, holding her head in his hands.

"What?" she smirked.

"Nothing." He resumed, his lips compressed against hers, their breath interlaced, their bodies locked.

David.

He pulled away again, this time, letting his hands fall out of her hair. He backed away from her, watching for any change. Something wasn't right.

"It didn't happen this way," he said, his hands raised in front of him, as if to block her appeal.

"It can."

"But it didn't. You left. You never came back. I've been living alone." He thought for a moment. "This isn't right. You're not real."

"David, I can be, we can be. I don't have to leave, I can stay."

"No, no Mel, you gotta go."

"Go where?" Her brow lifted. "Oregon?"

His insides trembled. The corners of her mouth rose up in ridiculing familiarity.

"Isn't that where you are? Some little forest in Oregon? Hmmm?" She was mocking him. Her joy from his fear. "Sitting on the ground in the middle of the night, awfully dangerous you know. Anything can happen, especially to someone who has fallen asleep." Before he could register her words she was on top of him. Her fingernails had grown long and they dug into the flesh under the collar of his shirt. Her face had rotted away to reveal a grinning skull with vampire teeth. She opened her hideous mouth and screamed into David's face.

He cried aloud, but no sound escaped.

David. Close your eyes.

He tried to focus on shutting his lids, but the ghoul screamed and screamed until David thought his eardrums would rupture. His blood was running over her fingers and with eager ferocity she dug her nails deeper into the collapsing flesh. His eyes would not close. The screams continued, the blood spit out of his veins. She pulled him closer, her hot breath filling his lungs. The creeping 'it' had shed Melissa's clothes and instead was covered in a grey cloak from which only its skinny, veiny, arms and tearing fingernails emerged. David could endure no more. Without thought or hesitation, David buried his head into the monster's cloak. The smell of decay ripped through his sinuses and was gone. He was in the forest again, his hands protectively gripped around his repeatedly scratched but otherwise unharmed throat. He slowly rose to his feet, checking and rechecking his body. A bush moved somewhere nearby and David whipped around. He couldn't see beyond the debris, but he knew what was coming.

   Lucas hadn't been able to pick up anything. He sat crouched on the forest floor for a few minutes before resigning. He didn't know where Masterson was and had only a faint pulse on Drake, let alone Emily. It wasn't until an hour later as he, unknowingly, walked in the opposite direction of David that he was suddenly hit with an image. He could see Masterson at the gate. He turned right (not left, Lucas thought with slight amusement) and descended down the embankment. He was sitting on the ground, looking at his hands, then his eyes slowly closed. He was sleeping! Lucas changed direction and broke into a run. Depending upon the dream, he might be able to reach Masterson before he woke, if he woke that was. It was no difference to Lucas if he killed David while taking his soul or if the angels did it while he dreamt. The rules were indiscriminate as long as a soul was rendered. He was getting anxious. Only a few hours left. He ran up the slope and across the drive then back down again. Masterson had been here. His presence was all over the tree limbs and stones that sat slightly disturbed on the ground. Lucas worked through the path, following David's steps, but his concentration was suddenly broken by a thudding noise in his ears. A heartbeat. David was close and he was running.

   The sound was followed by the faint, but distinct noise of footsteps working through the brush. David thought he could even vaguely make out Lucas' shape. He couldn't go this way any longer. If he trudged on Lucas would certainly catch up with him. David climbed the slope, his legs registering the laborious grade and speed at which he was pursuing it. Just shy of the embankment's edge David dropped to the ground pressing his back and legs flat against the hill. A small figure below was pushing aside branches and bushes along the gully floor. David's heart leapt frantically in his chest. His body heat was warming the earth under him and within seconds he could feel himself slowly sliding down the embankment. He dug his heels in, but they kept giving way to the layers of moss and mud that constructed the slope's surface. He was descending noticeably faster and faster. His fingers grasped at the cold earth, his scratches being torn wider and wider until his hands gave way and he fell the last fifteen feet. He hit the gully floor with rib cracking impact. His head and back were pressed into the giving ground. The air shot out of his lungs and he felt the cold rush of unconsciousness swim across his field of vision. His eyes rolled from side to side, noting the hovering trees, the looming embankment and then suddenly, a figure standing over him.

CHAPTER SEVENTEEN

*D*avid looked at the bare feet, their pale color almost glowing against the dark ground. His eyes began to focus, their view improving, but his head still felt drunk with haziness. The figure slowly kneeled beside him, her long brown hair brushing against her exposed forearms. She was, as before, dressed in a white gown that seemed to lie on her body rather than hang from it. She hunched there, her arms crossed over the tops of her knees, head tilted slightly so that they could make complete eye contact with each other. Her hair fell around her in a soft veil. Just the image of her soothed him and for a moment, his body didn't ache, nor his heart.

"David. Did you need me?"

"I fell. Thought you were him."

He should have felt compromised, lying there, face up to the sky, not a single movement while his predator gained ground, but he didn't. He felt calm. To him, she felt like peace.

"Yes, you have taken quite a fall. You're in pretty bad shape, which is why I am here. I want to know if you are ready."

"Ready for what?"

"For this."

She reached across the short distance between them and placed a cool hand on his chest. The sensation from her fingers was cold and grew stronger as it spread to the ends of each of his limbs. The soothing touch eased David's mind until it found his heart. Suddenly, he couldn't breathe. His heart was pumping fast, but no air remained in his lungs. He shuddered as the rhythmic beating took on a rapid succession of thudding in his chest. He looked with strained eyes at Rebecca who was watching, silently as his body twitched and spasmed. He grabbed her wrist, which instantly chilled his fingers.

"*Stooooop!*" he begged. She pulled her hand from his chest and he immediately felt the night air sweep past his mouth into his body. Gasping and coughing, he scrambled away from the white silhouette, but found he could only move a few inches.

"What the hell was that?"

"David-"

"No you tell me! Who are you?" He stared into her unearthly eyes and found the answer his body already knew. "No, no, I'm not ready! I'm only thirty-four years old, I can't!"

"David, you are badly hurt. If you stay here Lucas will catch you and not only will you die, but your soul will be trapped. If you come with me now, your body will die, but your soul will be free."

"What about Lucas? What about his deal, Mama Legna said-"

"If you come with me, Lucas will be given another fifty years on earth. When that fifty years is over he will, again, try to find a replacement. By then more rogue angels will be on his side. He won't make the same mistake twice. Next time, he will be successful and man will be at the mercy of powers much greater than himself."

David looked down at his body. Aside from Rebecca's personal illumination, the dark filled his vision and he couldn't see any injuries, but he had a feeling they were there.

"What's the damage?"

"You have broken five ribs and have bruised a couple of organs. Your left wrist is completely broken and you have a small concussion." He couldn't feel the pain. He couldn't feel anything, but her words made it real to him and his mind began to hallucinate a throbbing in his chest, wrist, and head.

"That isn't the worst of it, David," she leaned forward, her breath as cool as her touch. "When you wake, Lucas will be close, too close for you to run and he could sense it even if you did. You will have to face him, force him down. The only way you will be able to get down the mountain is if he sleeps."

"Sleeps? How do I do that?"

"You're smart, David. You must not let your doubt cloud your intellect. Focus. Focus and you might have a chance."

She rose to full posture and David thought she resembled a Diana sculpture. Her gown, though having lain on the mossy floor, was white and untouched and now was growing in length. David watched as her hem flowed from its ankle length, down over her feet and onto the ground. She wrapped her arms around her middle and across her chest.

"Time to go," she said.

"I can't."

"Are you sure? Pain is the only thing that awaits you."

"Have to try."

"It is your decision. I hope you are successful. May I tell you something, perhaps a word of encouragement?"

"I would be grateful," he could feel the pain creeping in and his body slowly awaking to its unwelcome presence.

"Your father has never left you. Whether in this life or the next, he will always find a way to be with you."

Her head slowly arched back, a slight sigh sounded and she was gone. Her disappearance left the forest even darker than before and once again David was overwhelmed by its vastness. He propped himself up on his palms, a sharp pain ripped from his wrist to his neck and he recoiled to the ground waiting for the fire to abate. The temperature had dropped since he left the house and the air had taken on a moisture that was only genuine to the early morning hours. A bit past midnight, he thought, but no later than one.

He rolled to his right, no doubt the side of his body without injury, and slowly crept up to his feet. His ribs, back and head seemed to throb in unison with his heartbeat. He touched his scalp and felt the warm presence of blood. He had really done it. He was truly screwed. So screwed that Death herself had found it appropriate to make a house call. She had been his way out and now, she, and his way out, were gone.

Her point had been simple enough, make Lucas sleep. There were a thousand ways human beings slept and twice as many reasons. David didn't think that it mattered how or why, but that unconsciousness was just as dangerous for Lucas as it was for him. It would give David the head start he needed to get to the highway and perhaps act as an opportunity for those who stalked around in dreams to have a go at his corrupted adversary. Either way, Lucas would be detained and David could make a run for it.

He thought a simple rock to the head would be sufficient. He didn't want to kill Lucas, having a death on his hands wouldn't make this nightmare any easier, but he wouldn't cry over making the asshole a vegetable either, a position, David thought, that would be fantastically ironic. He dragged his boot over the ground, searching for a substantial mound when one finally struck his steel toe. He gave it a concentrated kick, which shot it from the earth into a bush.

"Fuck." David dropped to his knees and reached under the dripping fern. His ribs jabbed and poked, his insides cringed. Hell isn't hot, he thought. Hell is cold and rainy and never sees sunlight. Who ever knew that it would actually be *north* of L.A? He scoffed at his own frustration and reached further until his hands fell upon a cold, round object. It was a rather smooth rock, worn down by centuries of hard weather, its size equating to that of a softball. Just big enough to do the job. He looked up at the slope from which he had dropped. He had not cleared the path along the gully floor because he had gone up and around it. If he cleared it, he would be able to determine where Lucas would come through right down to the last step. Time was running and he was in a lot of pain, but if he arranged the rocks and the logs just right . . .

Lucas had followed David's path along the gully for half an hour when he lost his mental track on his prey. It hadn't faded away, nor disappeared, but rather had simply stopped. Either Masterson was dead or blocking him. He didn't think Masterson knew enough to block him completely, but if he was dead one of *them* would certainly tell him. Christine wasn't the only one on his side, there were quite a few. Most of them were in hiding or trapped on mankind's plane, usually as children, but a small few were still free. A small few still stalked the dreamworld and they wanted Masterson dead more than Lucas did. If he died, they would tap Lucas to collect the soul and fulfill the pact. That was, if he was dead. The faint heartbeat that had once echoed so loudly told Lucas that Masterson was alive, struggling, perhaps injured, but alive all the same.

Lucas rested against a rock and reached into his pocket. His fingers closed around a three inch handle and pulled the knife from its storage. It was strange to him how specific the rules had been. Just as if he and Masterson were farmers back in the Dark Ages, it was decreed that should he fight and murder Masterson in life that it be by knife or sword. They were not permitted to use any advanced form of weaponry, which is why Drake had stripped Masterson's truck the evening following his arrival. No cheating. Lucas admired the sentiment and thought that if he was unable to defeat Masterson in a one on one fight, then he deserved whatever punishment the universe intended for him.

He ran his index finger over the edge of the blade

and watched in ambivalence as a small line broke his skin and began to bleed. The blood was black and barely visible in the night's shroud, but Lucas was entranced by its simple nature. Seeping from beneath the skin, warm and soft, little droplets fell from his hand to the ground while others made course down his finger, across the great plain of his palm. With every emerging bead came a small breath of freedom and Lucas rescinded his previous opinion of people who cut themselves. If his need for this feeling even surpassed his vanity, he would, as so many did, cut himself repeatedly to relieve the pressure, the struggle, to free the beast that crept inside his mind. The creature that crept inside the mind of every human being, big and dark with unforgiving eyes and an enraged mouth.

  He broke his fixation and pushed himself off of the rock. The heartbeat was a little louder now and he knew that Masterson was close. He wiped his hand on the back of his pants and resumed his path down the center of the gully. When he reached up to push aside a fallen branch, his eyes fell on the face of his watch. 1: 12 AM. He had been sitting on that rock for close to twenty minutes. Lucas' face grew hot. Someone was keeping him. Someone had held him in that state of fascination while Masterson raced toward the highway. They knew that little asshole would need all the help he could get. There wouldn't be any more stopping. He was going to kill that son of a bitch if he had to tear the whole goddamn forest apart. They couldn't help him. They couldn't protect him. They couldn't protect him from any of the dreamworld angels. Man was just a dumb animal with a soft spot, a toy for the evil that controlled the unconscious world. Lucas was once one of those toys, but Christine had helped him deviate from that servitude, work the system and pave the way for a new world. When this was all over, he was going to be a king in a new kingdom, strong, powerful, and free of any creature that might feed on his feelings and provoke his mind.

CHAPTER EIGHTEEN

Emily's eyes snapped open. She had felt the shift slightly, but now it seemed to be rushing through her. The solitary heartbeat was raging and behind it came a wave of darkness.

"Masterson. I know you are close, young David. Come out."

Lucas pushed aside fallen foliage, his boots sinking deep into the forest floor. His voice cut into the early morning and seemed to reverberate off the log next to which David lay, his body pressed stiffly into the embankment. He couldn't see him, but David knew that Lucas was but a few yards away. He would only have one shot, one lunge to swipe his head and then it would be up.

"Honestly, do you ever stop hiding, that is the reason I chose you, you know. So weak in so many ways. How could you let that amazing woman go? There she was, right in front of you, apologizing, and you off and broke it up. Damn fool. It doesn't matter if it is real," the volume of his voice was dropping. He knew he was close. "What really matters is that it is real to you. That's the whole point. If man lived inside his mind and in his dreams he would never hate, fear, or hurt ever again. In our dreams we are in control, not them. They told you to focus, didn't they? To be aware, be awake. Hard isn't it? Tiring. I used to believe that myself, used to think it was the answer to a good life. But it's not, mate. This is the answer. Give over your mind, forget this world, their world and become a part of a different one. Man could be stronger, man could have a say in what happens to him. David, you could have a say in what happens to your dad, to Brian, to Melissa." Lucas stopped and turned in a circle. David held his breath. "They took them away from you, can't you see that? It is all for nothing, it is all for them! What has this world ever done for you? You are so far gone that they can now penetrate your dreams, a place that is sacred to every human being, they have tainted it with monsters! You are a ruined man, Masterson. Your sad little life is over and where are they? Where is the goodness that is supposed to hold this universe together? How has it let these things happen to you? David, I know you can hear me and I know you are hurt. I will make it fast I promise you. The jump will be quick and your pain, minimal. I am offering to share my life with you, to share my mind and in the end we will die together and you will be free. We will both be free. We will control the universe, not the other way around. For the first time, our bodies will be free of our minds. Come out."

Lucas stared in the direction of the embankment. The darkness was still until suddenly a figure emerged. He was slightly hunched, limping and immediately Lucas could feel the strain his physical suffering was putting on his mind. His thoughts came through clear to Lucas, clear and strong.

"What you are doing is wrong, Jared."

"What *I* am doing? Your life is imprisoned by those who are *supposed* to protect you . . . I come along, want to set you free and my way is wrong? You're too blind to know-"

"I know that I don't want to be a part of what you are doing. I know that there is good in this world and that those who created it are being patient, helping man along, helping him to be better."

"Man is an animal. He does not evolve, his brutality does. He will always put his needs above others. He will always resort to violence as a way to fulfill those needs and through his stubborn refusal to achieve enlightenment, he is bringing forward some of the darkest times this world has ever known. Man has no business in the physical world, his mind is the only place he will find peace and reach the type of existence he so fervently craves."

"So what, give our souls to evil so that we can live in big houses with no walls, eat food with no taste, exist in a dream state that holds no true value? Cease as human beings? Reject the life that was given to us?"

"Not reject, simply acknowledge that you are in over your head. Man could never be grateful equivocally to the gifts he has been given. Man is not good enough to appreciate this world, nor will he ever flourish within it. Unconsciousness is the only state in which man proves to not be destructive, but rather contribute to the universe as a whole."

"Contribute? What?"

"With man gone to the outer planes of the universe, this earth bound world will need a new occupant."

"Angels?"

"Rogue angels are damned creatures locked into one plane or another, unable to tap their powers. After an eternity the punishment exceeds the crime. Your submission will release them onto this world where they will, for the first time in all creation, experience what man has so selfishly taken for granted. And I will be king among them."

"What will happen to the human race?"

"Sleep."

"Death?"

"No, sleep. Mankind will exist in slumber, forced to walk the vacated land of the dreamworld, alone. His soul finally experiencing the empty void his mind so desperately tried to ward off."

"I won't let you."

"Think you can stop me, warrior? Think I am the only human to know the touch of a fallen star? You are more wrong than you are naïve." He began to inch toward David and with each step his words grew heavier. "You will die, young David, die like the animal you are. No god is going to save you and no angel will come to your aid. The end is unavoidable."

"Mama will help me."

Lucas stopped, a small twitch rotated across his face, decreasing the intensity of his stare. "No, there is no one." The darkness held, but David could still sense Lucas' eyes racing back and forth in their sockets. He repressed his pain and stepped forward.

"Yes, there is. They came to me when I was in California and then again here. They say that you have violated the laws, that you are one of many to be used by the angels." He watched Lucas as best as he could, looking for holes. He sensed the break in Lucas' temperament and advanced. "Yes," he began again, ignoring shots of pain that raced through his body and into his brain. "There were some before you, stupid like you have been. Only difference is that they were successful." He permitted his sweat drenched face a small smile. He didn't know if Lucas could see it or not, but it didn't really matter. He certainly felt better.

"There has never been any one like me!" He was before David, their chests almost connecting before David had a chance to respond. "I could kill you."

"You could kill me and it wouldn't change the fact that you're being used." He laughed a little and felt his ribs pinch the soft tissue of his stomach. A warmth began to seep from its torn barrier. "You're a tool, Jared. Ha! A big ol' tool!"

Lucas grabbed David's collar and lifted him above the ground. The pressure of his forearms pressing against David's broken chest made a groan rise out of his throat and into the air where it evaporated into the cold. Lucas absorbed the painful noise and was contented by its honesty. He dropped David to the ground and hung over him, observing the grimace, the agony and the smell of death that had come to rest on David's shattered body. His eyes were closed.

"The pain is too much for you," he said, sitting back

on his heels. "This world is too much, young David. And you have fought a good fight." He reached back into his pocket, found the knife's handle and turned just as David brought the rock crashing into his head. The blow took every ounce of strength he had, but the job was done. Lucas lay, nearly face down in the damp earth. David had felt his skull give under the weight of the stone. If David didn't make it down the mountain he was certain they would both die, Lucas maybe even before then.

He worked off his fleece and then the t-shirt beneath it. He put the long sleeve fleece back on and wrapped Jared's head in the sweat covered cotton. Every movement hurt. He was sure that additional damage had been done just by pushing himself off the bank, but if his conscience was to be clear, a little more pain would have to be endured. He slowly brought himself to his feet. His head felt as if it were at the top of the Himalayas. He swayed a minute, waiting for the wooziness to pass. He looked around, but the spots in his vision made the ground look polka-dotted and black. He stepped forward and nearly tripped over a tree limb. It would do. He leaned over and the world went white.

"Can't," he said and then pinched the side of his abdomen. His body registered the punishment and the forest came back into focus. He grabbed the branch and dragged it to where Lucas lay. He hunched over the body, lifted Lucas' head with his good hand and placed the limb beneath it. The elevation wasn't much, but David felt it was still more than Lucas deserved. He checked the figure's pulse and found it to still be thumping.

"Hmpf, too bad." His voice was dry and hoarse, but it sounded overwhelming in the silence. He negotiated his way to his feet again and waited for the pain, but it didn't come. His body was shutting down and numbness was beginning to work its magic.

"Thank god."

"Don't tank him just yet," an old voice replied. There she was, small and gentle, carpetbag in hand. "You're in bad shape, boy. Somethin' awful, I'd say."

"Mama, you've come to help me,"

"No, you know I can't."

"Then what? Either help or go away."

"Don't take dat tone wit me, boy I don save you more den you know. I's just come to say dat you're four miles from da highway."

"Four miles? I can't walk four miles, I can barely stand here!"

"Not a question. Walk four miles you must, besides, he only gonna sleep an hour or so, then up and after you he come."

"No freakin' way, I bashed his fucking head in!"

"Shoulda bashed harder." Her tone was calm and simple, her demeanor strong and unwavering.

"What should I do?"

"Walk. Dat's all. Just walk. The gully will show da way. Take his knife, still a few branch here and dhere."

"Everything hurts."

"Never mind dat. C'mon, off you go. Four miles ain't goin' to cover itself."

He grabbed the knife and trudged his way past Mama Legna and back onto the path of the ravine's floor.

"I believe in you, boy."

He turned to see her, but once again, she was gone. He took what he hoped to be his last glance of Jared Lucas.

"Asshole."

As before, he didn't know if Lucas could hear him, but David felt better.

CHAPTER NINETEEN

The trees. That is what the creature had told him, *the trees.*

"What fucking trees?"

Martin paced the well lit confines of his home's downstairs den. Every light between the master bedroom and the den was on. He felt as he used to when he was young, as if he were the only one left in the world. Everyone else was asleep and he was alone in the dark and quiet.

He collapsed into his desk chair, his bathrobe coming to rest over his knees and onto the floor. The desk itself was beautiful, a gift from his parents after he made editor at *Wolf.* There were stacked manuscripts, a magazine article, unopened mail and a small pile of messages from work that he hadn't even glanced at. The picture above the article depicted a slightly chubby, completely hammered pop star climbing into a SUV. The headline read: Making A Break For It, Busty and Busted. Martin smirked. The article had actually been a promo for the pop queen's new album, but instead of attending a benefit for The Haven Music Foundation, the diva had gone clubbing. Martin had sent his photographer instead of a reporter and they ran the story two days ahead of schedule. He didn't particularly care for the gossip section of his magazine, the honest and approved interviews were better anyway, but the sleaze sold copies and after only a year of being an editor he was forced to extend the section to three pages. He flipped the article over, taking note of a few grammatical mistakes and perused the remaining sections. There, just above the end of the page a headline read: The Heart of Music Finds A Light Peace In The Trees Of Oregon. The article was the last piece *Wolf* had done on

Lucas, just prior to his seclusion. The words seemed to stare back at Martin; Light, Heart, Peace, Trees.

Martin bolted from his chair into the kitchen where his keys, sun glasses and cell phone sat on the counter in their usual place. He grabbed the red phone. His hands shook with impatience and twice he scrolled passed David's number. When his fingers finally found it, he pressed *send*. The volume didn't seem loud enough. He switched the call to speaker and heard the ring echo in the tiled room. Two rings, three, four, six, nine, twelve rings and no voicemail. Martin slowly closed the phone. He stared into the dark.

He had sent him. David had asked why and Martin didn't have an answer, he had just sent him.

His feet found their purpose and five minutes later Martin was dressed, in the car and on his way to the airport.

There were no flights out of LAX until 6:00 and Martin figured Ontario would be his best bet. Morning rush hour was seven hours off and Martin made the eighty mile drive in fifty minutes. He parked his car in long term parking and hopped on the airport shuttle. He didn't know what he was going to find in Oregon. His bag fell against his leg as the shuttle took a hard right and he jumped at the unsuspecting weight of it. No, he didn't know what was in those trees, but he felt certain it wasn't good.

David's legs felt wobbly. The pain in his head had abated, but his ribs ached and every step brought unconsciousness swimming across his vision. He stopped at a clearing and let his head roll back between his shoulder blades. His eyes looked up and through the height of unified trees, found a breach of sky poking through the thick branches. There it was, the outside world. He was not as far from it as he had felt. The few stars beamed in their heavenly field, their light reached his pupils with intense extravagance.

"Please. . . Help me."

The stars replied not, but instead twinkled in sincere obligation. They were not hope, but rather a mere reminder of a place he would never see again. A home that would sit unoccupied aside from an unattended cat who would starve in its owner's absence. The stars paralleled the light in her voice, which he would forever be without, his ineptitude wrapped in its velvet tone. Those stars were the confirmation of his unimportance. The world had forgotten him. David didn't notice his eyes close, but when his body hit the ground, his ribs finally gave way and his mind, drunk with pain, went blank.

The field was dark, he knew that much. The soil was dry and seemed to reflect the only light around him aside from the stars overhead. David rose to his feet and felt no pain. His body felt whole, but absent in the odd void where he currently stood, surrounded by tilled dirt and a black sky. He wondered if he was dead, wondered if it was over. He turned in a circle, taking in the landscape. He seemed to be standing in a barren field between two forests. He was alone.

"Hello?"

The air was stagnant and it was with a sudden surprise that David felt the rush of a breeze. He turned his face upward to embrace it, but instead his eyes caught the shapes of four soaring figures. As their forms became more clear to David, their cries reached his ears.

"Daaaaaviiiiiiid," they chimed, each voice carrying a higher pitch than the one before it. Again and again they screeched, "Daaaaaviiid! We've come for you!" They were dropping height and were almost level to the field.

David ran. He ran for the trees. He ran as quickly as his legs would carry him and yet, the forest grew no closer. His head craned over his shoulder only to see that the banshees were almost on top of him. A jagged nail snagged the flesh connecting his shoulder to his neck.

"Piece by piece," the shrill voice said from behind him. "Sleeping, young David is sleeeeeeping!"

He was. He had finally fallen asleep and now he was somewhere lost, running for his life from creatures that were reaching and ripping with every touch.

"Rebecca! Mama! Help!"

His voice seemed to only travel a short distance in the thick air.

"Can't help you," the creatures squealed, "nobody here for you!"

Their mocking voices caressed the back of his neck, the ground thundered under his pounding footsteps and then his legs gave beneath him.

"Wake up, wake up, wake godammit!" He had to convince himself. They had landed and were walking toward him. Their faces were contorted in pleasured grimaces.

"Piece by piece," they chanted.

"Wake up, wake up!"

"Come to get you."

Close your eyes.

David slammed his eyelids shut.

CHAPTER TWENTY

David looked at the surrounding forest and ironically found comfort in its return. The pain had also returned. His head throbbed in cadence with his heartbeat and everything below his neck felt tight with bloated agony. His fall had destroyed his already cracked ribs and his lungs were carrying their broken weight. He rose, as did the pain. Each breath thick with fluid that seemed to be filling his lungs, his body seemed to cry in small shudders that shook his frame and brought fresh lines of heat racing to his temples. He was dying. He knew it. The fall was the last straw and now he was going to die alone, here in the woods. Jared Lucas had been right; he was, once again, in over his head.

His feelings of self pity began to press down on his weakened shoulders and David, exhausted and beaten to his end, wanted nothing more than to lay down upon the forest floor and breath in the damp coolness for the last time. He looked longingly to the ground, but his gaze was interrupted by distant movement. He narrowed his eyes, straining to focus through the trees and into the gloom. Something was running parallel to David's position and its speed was slowed by the distance between them. It looked to him as if it was-

He heard a scream. It was the high pitched, unified squeal of the creatures from his dream. They were here, in the woods, real. He stumbled backward. What had happened? He tried to think. He had fallen asleep. They had chased him down, then the voice said to close his eyes. The voice.

"Are you there?" The words came out in a soft whisper, but David still felt they were too loud. In confirmation of his fear, one of the flying creatures changed direction and began to soar towards David, the other three screaming wretchedly behind it.

"Please," he said. He waited, trying to shake off the image of the figures getting closer. They would no doubt spot him soon. Then the answer came and with its arrival David felt a tinge of resentment.

Run.

When he was younger, David would go for runs late at night to relieve the tension and often confusing melodrama that seemed to plague his close knit family. After they had all gone to sleep, David would quietly sneak out into the night and run the nearby neighborhoods of the suburbia in which he lived. After a while two miles turned into four, four into six and a twice a week exercise regiment became a daily requirement. With the small exception of a couple of years as an undergrad, David carried the habit into his twenties and frequently racked up over thirty miles a week.

This, however, was not suburbia. He was not sixteen. And the creatures that were chasing him made his relative woes seem nonexistent in comparison. But, somehow in some way, the two coincided. His pain, his disappointment, his inability to understand, his physical agony combined with his failure thus far to get out of the woods, all seeped together and brought David a rush of rage that he before had never felt. He began to run and as he did, images flashed through his mind and across his vision.

Melissa, lying in bed on her side, silently crying while David slept, unaware, beside her. He raced up the embankment, over a fallen tree and back down to the ravine again.

Brian, crouched beneath a pine, his knees against his chest, his face pale with pneumonia . . . "Don't think I'm gonna make it, man." He had been so scared.

The screams were getting closer, the dreamy

illumination on the horizon signaling that the dawn was near.

His dad working in the garage, standing in front of the work bench, whistling as his fingers negotiated a washer from a bolt.

David was coughing now. His chest was pitching the morning air in and out of his lungs, but his legs never slowed.

He could see Drake, sitting in the back of the Durango, eyes level and kind, then a small smile crossing his face.

He was running straight downhill now and below he could see a break in the trees.

Lucas. Standing in front of the fireplace, his arm stretched across the length of the mantle, his head dropped down below his shoulders, his body black against the rising flames.

David broke into the image and felt himself running toward Lucas, toward the fireplace and at last connecting with Lucas' midsection as they both fell into the fire. The scene filled David's vision. He could feel the fire's heat ripping through his flesh, its blinding light burning his eyes, and then the darkness washed over him.

CHAPTER TWENTY-ONE

*V*oices.

"Wick, look. Is he alive?"

"Barely. Alex, go back to the camp and get help. Eric, give me your sleeping bag. If we hurry we might be able to save him."

David didn't see anything at first, but heard a beeping noise long before he could open his eyes. When his eyelids finally parted, he saw that a room had replaced the forest and in lieu of trees, a bed, chair and TV now compiled his surroundings. He had monitors on each side, which began to announce his heartbeat's increased pace. A blonde nurse hustled into the room.

"Well, hey. There you are. How are you feeling?"

She pressed a few buttons here and there, but never broke eye contact with him. Green, he thought with relief, she has perfectly natural, beautiful green eyes.

"Better, I guess. Where am I?"

"Legacy Emmanuel Hospital. You were transferred here from Hood yesterday."

"Hood." He looked at the woman, her smile wide and comforting. He had made it off the mountain. "Who brought me in?"

"From the trail, you mean? A professor and a group of students out camping. Lucky for you he knew what he was doing. Your injuries are pretty extensive. I'll page your doctor."

She left him, her white coat flying out behind her as she walked back into the hall. He let his head fall back onto the pillow.

"Made it,' he said aloud.

"Sure did," a voice replied. Mama Legna sat in the chair beside the window, carpet bag on her lap, hands neatly folded.

"Thought you'd forgotten about me."

"Oh no, never, boy. We are always watching you, especially the boss. She helped you those last few moments now, didn't she?"

"Who?"

"You know, the head beauty, chief of our world."

"God?"

"Dat's right."

"But nobody helped me. I was alone in that forest with those crazy screaming things chasing me! I called and nobody answered!"

"She most certainly did! What, you too stupid to not know when a voice don't belong to ya?"

She was leaning toward him now, and he, gripped in the sudden realization of her question, propped himself up on his elbows.

"Emily?"

She smiled.

"She was the one talking to me?"

"Dat's right."

"But, why didn't she help me, then? Why did she let Jared do all of these things, let him almost kill me? Let me almost kill myself?"

"What dar you on 'bout? She never told you to kill yerself! Dat day in the shower, dat was all you! Ain't nobody to blame for dat, but yer foolish self!"

"She's just a girl, she isn't God."

"Oh, you so sure now."

"No, I'm not."

"Listen boy," she got up from the chair and walked to his bedside. Her small wiry fingers wrapped themselves around his right hand. "Sometimes it tis better not to know. A gift is a gift. She was dhere. She got you out. You alive because she help you. Dat's all. Dat's all dhere needs to be. I'm goin' now." She picked up her bag and moved towards the door. "You've done a good thang, David. Go be happy now. She wil' handle da rest."

Before he could reply she was gone. Somewhere, amid the broken bones and scratches, David knew that it was over.

Horatio's fur seemed to glow in the sunlight that drenched his favorite windowsill. He lay on his side, undisturbed by David's entrance into the apartment. The super had come by on and off for a week to feed Horatio and check on David's place, while David had recovered in Oregon. Just the picture of his beloved pet made David feel like crying in relief. He had been certain that he would never see this space or Horatio ever again. He dropped his keys onto the couch and bee-lined for the window. Horatio stretched his toes in slight recognition, but his eyes remained shut. David kneeled before the animal and placed his cheek on the rising and falling belly of fur. A small purr began from inside the soft bulge. David stroked Horatio's head and tenderly scratched the underside of his ears. The feline's head rolled in direction, to the left and then downward. David closed his eyes, allowing a wet drop of gratitude to fall into the bristled orange terrain. When David's hand came to rest on the sill, Horatio's paw reached out to cover it. The gesture was so kind, so deliberate, that it felt as if it was human. He looked into the green eyes that were still and soft and another tear found its way out and down.

"Almost didn't make it, boss." Horatio rested his chin on his paw that still resided over David's hand. His eyes gradually closed. David sat, unmoving for the next hour, trying to absorb this moment of good. He pushed away the last three days, letting Horatio's pleasant hum fill his head and after a time began to believe his life would return to him.

A FEW MONTHS LATER

David sat in his office and looked out onto the golden landscape. The palms stood tall and unwavering, but a small breeze brought the ocean air in through his windows. It was sunny and clear, his favorite kind of day.

"Knock, knock," Martin poked his head in from behind the mahogany door. "Got Jane's piece on the award show. Seems to work, but I wanted you to give it a second look."

"'Okay."

"And a messenger just dropped off the last of your escrow papers, which you are, by the way, fucking crazy for signing."

"Oh yeah, why is that?"

"Are you kidding? Aside from the fact that you nearly died up there and that that house is probably packed with worse juju than even your spiritual highness could clear? Yeah, I'd say you're off your fucking rocker."

"You wouldn't understand, Martin."

"Look, I know you went through some crazy shit with Lucas. And I know it was my fault that you were stuck up there."

"It wasn't anybody's fault-"

"Just let me finish, alright? My dreams have stopped, no more faces in mirrors, so I know you must be safe, but that doesn't mean you're okay and it doesn't mean that they can't come back for you."

"Martin, I know, believe me, I know, but trust me when I say that they're done with me. Even if there was another star . . . Whoever *they* are, they're done."

"I'm just sayin' . . . live in that house? I mean, why, David? It's strange enough that he left everything to you, but that doesn't mean you have to live there."

"Only part time. Half here, half there. I gotta get past this and besides, the house is gorgeous-"

"So sell the damn thing! I mean, for fuck's sake,

Dave! Take the millions he left you and buy a place near downtown, but don't go living up on Hood alone in that freak shack."

"So, come up with me. You could use a break from Virginia and we can get some work done."

"Hell no. Jesus Christ couldn't get me back on that mountain. It was bad enough having to go up there to ID Lucas, find you half dead in a hospital and walk the cops through the house to collect your stuff. No, no, no fucking way. Thank you, but piss off."

"Alright, but if you change your mind," he took the papers out of the envelope, scratched his signature across the bottom of three pages. "I'll be leaving in the morning on the 9:00 AM flight."

"Whatever asshole, be safe," he opened the door, took one last look at his fellow editor and closed it behind him.

It wasn't raining, but the air was still stiff with moisture. He passed the gates and drove slowly up the drive, parking beneath the carport. He exited the suburban and went around the back to get his bags. He unloaded the back seat, grabbed two suitcases and walked up the steps to the front door, which he was not surprised to find was unlocked. He set the bags down, sighed at the facade and descended down the hallway into the den. Despite the abundance of late morning light outside, the room was dark with the exception of one light that Drake had turned on.

"Welcome back."

"Thanks, Drake. Is Emily-"

"Oh no, she left after you were taken to the hospital."

"Left?"

"Well, left in the way deities do," he smiled. "Would you like to know what happens next?"

"Didn't come all this way for nothing," David returned the smile.

"Of course. Well, it's quite simple really. We have assigned you to a fallen star not far from here. She is communicating with a rogue angel, they haven't quite figured it out yet, but they will. She has already tapped a prospect, a young man from Siberia, but he doesn't arrive until tomorrow."

"Okay. Any last minute advice?"

"No, as an angel, you'll know what to do. The battle rages on. Know what I mean?"

"Yeah, I get it."

"Ready?"

"As I'll ever be."

Drake guided David to a chair. The cushions were dense and the leather covering them was cold, very cold. He placed his arms on each side of the chair, palms down and let his fingers hang over the edge. Drake walked around behind him and placed two warm hands on either side of David's head. David's right index finger curled in and found a broken seam in the chair's arm. *Think of that*, he thought, *focus on the seam and not what's about to happen.*

"Death is just one step in any man's existence, David."

He fingered the seam and felt a prick of pain rush his fingertip. He glanced downward and saw a thin green object sticking out of the chair.

"It comes for everyone."

It was a pine needle. Pine needle. Cold cushions. Dark room.

"And now, young David it has come for you."

Jared Lucas jerked his hands violently to one side. David's sleeping mind screamed and then there was nothing.

THE END

DANAE SAMSON

will return with her next novel

BURN: THE CASUAL SLAUGHTERS OF SIMON GREEN

MediaAria CDM
www.mediaaria-cdm.co.uk

Lament Hill

THE COMPETITION

If you enjoyed reading Danae Samson's 'Lament Hill', enter our competition by completing the entry form, which can be found on the 'From The Publisher' page on our website and win an exclusive 'Jared Lucas Lives' T-shirt and cap set.

The Competition Question:
What is the name of David Masterson's Editor at Wolf Magazine?

The deadline for responses is 1st June 2012 and the winner will be announced on our wesite later in the month.

Other **MediaAria CDM** titles
available from all good online bookstores.

COLD TALES
IN THE SHADOW OF THE COLD WAR
by
C D Mick

VATARI CHRONICLES:
THE BENFEADH
by
GAY ANNE HOLLYWELL

A ROCKER'S CHORUS
by
C D Mick

SIGN OUR PETITION

For a *Rights For Nature* Bill*
which can be found on the
New Energy Society (NES)
page of our website
www.mediaaria-cdm.co.uk

CLIMATE CHANGE
AFFECTS US **ALL**.

YOU CAN MAKE A DIFFERENCE.

MAKE A DIFFERENCE
TODAY

*UK NATIONALS ONLY.
USA NATIONALS CAN FIND A SAMPLE LETTER TO WRITE
TO THEIR CONGRESSMAN ON THE NES WEB PAGE.

If you have enjoyed reading Lament Hill, stay informed, be entertained and join MediaAria CDM on Facebook or Twitter and interact with the Author online.

To read more about all our books and to buy them, visit www.mediaaria-cdm.co.uk. You will also find information on author interviews and news of any author events, competitions and company initiatives.

MediaAria CDM

ENJOY THE SITE!